TO SAMATHA, Alyssa,
AND DANIELLA

Cliff Falls

A novel by C. B. Shiepe

Believe!

CBE

D0802175

CLIFF FALLS MEDIA · LOS ANGELES, CA

CLIFF FALLS

BY C.B. SHIEPE

www.clifffalls.com

Published by Cliff Falls Media, 2275 Huntington Drive, Suite 420,
San Marino, CA 91108 * office@clifffallsmedia.com

International Standard Book Number: 978-0-9827020-0-0
Library of Congress Control Number: 2010904260

Printed in the United States of America

First Edition, May 2010

Cover design: Sean Teegarden and Jane Moon. Typesetting: Jane Moon.
Author photo: Pam McComb.

"C.B. Shiepe has struck a cord. In Cliff Falls *author Shiepe has found a story-telling device that captures the core of the 'former child star' syndrome, creating a spell-binding tale that keeps you interested from start to surprising finish. I sat up through the dark hours reading this book. It kept me turning the pages…and filled me with a sense of hope. As a man who has lived and collected thousands of genuine kid star stories, I highly recommend this illuminating and insightful work."*
   – Paul Petersen, Founder, A Minor Consideration

"A fast, cinematic read, I recognized myself in Cliff Falls. *I didn't grow up as a child star or a famous preacher's kid, but when I laughed out loud, it was a laugh of recognition. You will find your own story told here too, especially if you were the football player pressured to complete plays, the A student with love measured by school grades, or the bookworm facing a daily quiz at the dinner table…. C. B. Shiepe has captured that experience and married it to our celebrity-centric culture. This entertaining, insightful book is the engaging result."*
   – Charles Slocum, Writers Guild of America, West

"A stunningly visual journey told with wit and humor that is anchored with a big heart and tons of soul. Cliff Falls *reads with ease and confidence, and has dialogue as fresh as your last conversation."*
   – Sarah Skibitzke, Emmy-Award winning producer

*"*Cliff Falls *is a marvelous and deeply profound book that touched my heart and the very depths of my soul. For some of us, even though we are adults, we are still children seeking the confidence and courage to realize our deepest longings: fulfilling our dreams and making a difference in our own lives and those we touch. This compelling story illustrates the power of hope and a childlike faith to overcome adversity."*
   – June Scobee Rodgers, Ph.D., wife of Space Shuttle Challenger Commander, and Founding Chairman, Challenger Center

●

This book was written for an audience of One

And dedicated to my Mom, Marie Anne Shiepe,
for her gifts of belief, strength and unconditional love

And to all who struggle, in and out
of the spotlight, to know their belovedness

Chapter One

"It's one thing to believe in something when you don't need it to be true. It's another when everything is riding on it."
– The Ghost Writer

AUGUST 16, 1987

Heavy smoke could be seen from miles away. It covered the street filled with fire trucks and police cars. Twenty-three structures lay in ruin. The dry rot and plastic sets had burned quickly. Light from the fire flickered across the faces of the gathering crowd of overnight studio employees watching the firefighters extinguish the blaze.

A studio golf cart sped to the scene, stopping short of the makeshift barricade. Two men stepped out, one larger than the other. They wore *Little Guy Mike* black satin jackets, embossed in gold thread; one said "assistant director" and the other "producer."

The men shielded their mouths and noses from the toxic smoke as they ducked under the plastic yellow tape, their eyes glaring upward at what remained, the rising metal scaffolding exposed through smoldering chunks of torched foam rubber. It was all that separated the front from the back, the outside from the inside. They stared into the structure as the smoke cleared, horrified by the mangled tower of *Little Guy Mike* merchandise glowing in the distance.

"We found a pile of this stuff," a firefighter shouted, holding a charred lunch box.

The two men glanced at each other knowing the day had come.

"This was no accident," the firefighter said, returning to the blaze.

"When I get my hands on him…" the imposing assistant director muttered. Burt Cummings was an intimidating figure, which, from the studio's perspective, was a benefit on set, but his short fuse always caused more problems than it solved.

"Calm down," the producer insisted, attempting to keep Burt in line.

"He just killed the show," Burt said under his breath knowing that the show and his job were over. Not only was the set destroyed, but once the public discovered the origins of the fire, they would not be able to separate *Little Guy Mike* from the crazed teenager who struck the match.

The Fire Chief ordered them to move back.

Stepping away, the producer focused his attention on damage control. "We can still save the syndication," he said to Burt. The money was in repeats, mining the show's nine-year history. Internationally, they were already being dubbed in Japanese, French and Italian. The lawyers were now in final negotiations, drawing up contracts. The producer would have to think quickly to save this ship from sinking. Turning to an enraged Burt, he was adamant, "No one can find out who started this."

"Don't let him get away with this," Burt fumed.

"Don't worry, he'll pay."

* * *

SIX HOURS EARLIER...

Clay was perched precariously above the studio backlot, above the hanging cables and darkened floodlights. His acid-wash jeans and faded U2 t-shirt under a nylon jacket were his only shield from the night wind. But he didn't care.

It was not unusual for him to return after dark, ascend the rusty scaffolding, and find refuge in what he heard, but this night was different. He didn't have to wait for the words to come, they arrived on their own. They poured out...out of his being, out of his heart... out of his pen...howling like the intensifying Santa Ana winds that swept against his face...that ruffled his dyed black hair.

With ink-stained fingers, he wrote it all down. Every word, just as he heard it, he wrote it down.

...scared children — all of us — dealing with adult things — wondering if we are that strong. And everyone wants us to be someone or something else....

The voice knew how he felt. It always did. How it felt when people thought they owned a piece of you; how it felt when your every move was captured on camera or in print. How it felt when there was a self out there being marketed that wasn't you.

He told himself that he didn't care about anyone or anything, but he did care. He hated that. He wished he could shut that part of himself down, but that was easier said then done.

Leaning back against the crude metal pipes that supported the hollow structure, he clenched the flapping pages in his hand as he wrote. He wrote about every fear... every expectation as the one phrase repeated in his spirit.

...scared children — all of us — dealing with adult things — wondering if we are that strong. And everyone wants us to be someone or something else....

His green eyes glanced up from the page for a moment as his legs dangled off the plywood ledge. This was the backside of the façade, the ugly side — his refuge.

For nine seasons and counting, the exterior of the

structure was the symbol of the typical American home life. The happy existence the show perpetuated, he never knew. The house itself was idyllic, but hollow. The white foam clapboard sparkled like freshly polished teeth. Empty pillars only appeared to support the stylized arch made of plywood and rubber. The yard was well manicured, though closer inspection revealed plastic flowers and trees propped up by wooden braces.

Over the years, the exterior had been painted many times, its red shutters and foam clapboard well maintained. But the inside remained the same, a dusty dumping ground of empty paint cans and discarded props. It was messy and murky, a place not created for the camera.

The backside had been sort of a clubhouse, with him as the only member. This was the one place he would return. It was the only place he could disappear, even for just a few moments. He felt safe here. He always did. Even on this night.

Glancing below, the smoldering fire was nearly out. What had he done?

He had waited his whole life for his eighteenth birthday, believing that something would change. Nothing was ever going to change.

He never knew the difference between a normal childhood and this. He started at 11-months-old, working commercials and print ads after winning a contest in his hometown. He was still waiting for those pinchable cheeks to lean out. His earliest memories were of going on auditions with his mom. It was fun then, and they would always go for ice cream afterwards. That was the last time he felt normal. Gripping the pen, he knew he was always trying to get back to that place of feeling normal.

The world envied him, but he would trade shoes in a heartbeat with any of the kids outside the gate. Growing up on the lot, he could see them in the park across the street playing with their parents and wished his days were as ordinary as that.

His mom was supposed to fly in today. She never showed. Since he was 12, his mom hadn't even been in the picture — except for when the show was on hiatus or a few visits throughout the year. He could never forgive her for leaving him with them.

All they cared about was money. He was sure if he died, they'd find a way to sell tickets to his funeral. They'd probably do a joint promotion with a candy company and stick a few golden tickets in chocolate bars. Even in death they'd find a way to exploit him. He didn't care about the money and besides, he never saw it. What he did fear was selling out, not for the cash, but to please people. Everyone loved "Little Guy Mike," but no one cared about him.

His eyes returned to the page. He had believed that things would get better, that things would change even though everything around him told him different.

He was supposed to get the day off. It would have been his first in five weeks. He had spent the last few months touring packed stadiums with that anti-drug campaign to help bolster his image. In their eyes, protecting his image was clearly more important than any reality he lived with.

Instead, he spent the day signing autographs at a press event to please the studio. That's when he found out his mom wasn't coming. Some excuse about feeling out of place. He felt like an idiot. He couldn't believe that after everything, he had actually been looking forward to her showing up. At eighteen he thought he'd be over all this… that he'd feel like an adult, but he just felt like that same overwhelmed kid.

He was tired of all the things he had to care about… the advertisers, studio executives, the audience, his image, and everyone else's expectations. He didn't want to care about anyone else but himself anymore. Besides they were never happy anyhow.

All he knew was that he had this desire to have control, to get it all back, to take back every false perception of who they said he was. Just for a day he wanted the inside and the outside to be the same.

On this, his eighteenth birthday, it was time. He had finally said no, and he said it again and again that day.

He said it as he stormed off the set, past the colossal *Little Guy Mike* cake that was melting under the blistering lights, the discolored frosting blurring the portrait. Everything inside of him told him to keep walking.

He said it outside the art deco commissary as he tore from the stucco wall a poster of "Little Guy Mike" pointing his finger like Uncle Sam. The bold lettering read "Just Say No!" and he did.

He said it as he reached under the dash and hot wired a

nearby studio tram and sped off the lot.

He said it as he raced through Toys R Us, sweeping *Little Guy Mike* merchandise off the shelves — the dolls, board games and lunch boxes spilling into the empty cart.

At the cash register, the checker's perplexed expression said it all as each beep increased the total — $857.23 *beep*, $885.74 *beep*, $907.88 *beep*. Pausing, the clerk cautiously looked up and asked, "Could I get an autograph?"

"No!"

He said "no" in the parking lot as he popped each sparkling Mylar balloon that bared his marketable face. "No! No! No!"

And he said it at the news stand, tearing his smiling face in two, manually separating the *Teen* from the *Beat*, Kirk Cameron from Ricky Schroeder.

When the angry clerk objected, he promptly handed him a credit card. The clerk glanced at the name in disbelief. "Are you kidding me?" But he wasn't kidding and pointed to a rack filled with *TV Guide* magazines. The caption read "18 at Last!" The clerk swiftly placed the magazines into a *Little Guy Mike* pillowcase Clay held open.

And he said it into the night, as the studio tram, overflowing with *Little Guy Mike* merchandise, raced down the historic back lot, winding through the façade-lined streets, accelerating past the timber-framed structures, the famed sets from television and motion pictures. Finally, the tram stopped. A "Little Guy Mike" doll with a noose around its neck dangling from the rear view mirror.

Stepping off the tram, Clay gathered as much as he

could carry and then approached the *Little Guy Mike* set. With arms filled, he carried the contents through the bright red door with polished brass knocker, to the outside patch of dirt on the other side of the façade. Back and forth he went, tirelessly piling item upon item.

The tram nearly emptied, he retrieved the last box, a "Little Guy Mike" Halloween costume, the cardboard perimeter decorated with playful images of the boy. He stared at the plastic mask suffocating beneath the thin layer of cellophane. Taking it out, he held it up against the night sky, the moonlight illuminating its cut-out eyes. The contoured face with rouge cheeks was anything but natural, the forced expression of a mischievous child haunting. He hated this mask.

Clay placed the plastic mask, face up, on top of the great mound of *Little Guy Mike* merchandise. Then he struck a match.

The plastic mask slowly melted as the flames spread. Toxic fumes filled the air.

His youthful face basked in the orange glow of the blaze, his green eyes staring blankly into the fire. He was done. He had nothing left to say and that was why he was surprised when the words came.

... scared children — all of us — dealing with adult things — wondering if we are that strong. And everyone wants us to be someone or something else....

Consumed with this truth, he ascended the scaffolding

and began scribbling away as the fire died out below.

Lost in his thoughts, he barely noticed that the night wind had become more pronounced, like the words streaming out of his soul. The Santa Ana was invigorating—and like all things that made him feel alive— it was also dangerous. A danger he didn't realize until it was too late, until the reignited embers filled the air and his papers took flight.

The gale-force winds shook the structure. Gripping the jagged beams, he climbed down the scaffolding, removed his jacket and beat it hopelessly against the emboldened flames. But they continued to mount, crawling up the side of the façade, rising like shameful prayers finally released.

He froze for what seemed an eternity, realizing that the fire was out of control. After making his way through the front door, he turned back, his glossy eyes taking one last look at the show's set. The façade was rapidly turning black, the entire structure was on fire, and worse, it was spreading.

As the backlot burned, Clay Grant ran into the night.

Chapter Two

"Sometimes a picture is worth more than a thousand words," the photographer thought, removing the extended lens from his Minolta. Placing it securely in the camera bag, he glanced briefly across the room at *Entertainment Now* on the Colorado motel television set. It was the weekend edition hosted by Kat Stone.

"He was America's guy as the star of the 80's sitcom hit Little Guy Mike, *about the antics of a lovable orphan. Then he disappeared the same night a mysterious fire on the show's set burned down the studio's historic backlot. Whatever happened to Clay Grant?"*

The man tossed the empty suitcase on the mattress and opened it.

Nauseous from the altitude, he sat down momentarily

on the side of the bed, his eyes returning to the television.

"Although an official studio investigation did not link Clay to the fire, he disappeared from the public eye and later from Uncle Sam — reportedly owing the IRS over four hundred thousand dollars in back taxes."

Standing up, he started packing, knowing that interest in Clay had not faded in the years since the fire. There was still a market for the former child star and this photographer was betting on it. He tossed his toiletries in the suitcase, along with two towels from the motel bathroom.

"It seems everyone is looking for this missing star on the run. In this ENZ exclusive, our reporters tracked down Clay's last hiding place in Beaver Creek, Colorado and spoke with his former landlady."

The photographer stopped packing, went to the television and turned up the volume. Crouching down, his attention was solely glued to the screen. He didn't intend to be on television, but was surprised the crew captured him taking pictures in the distance.

Burt Cummings shook his head as he recognized himself in the shot, right in the middle of the reporter and landlady in her terrycloth bathrobe. There he was, camera flashing, silently taking pictures in the background, like an eager extra attracting more attention than the principle. Despite the extra twenty pounds, he thought he looked good on television. Not bad for fifty-two. He was quick to ignore the thinning hair and wide forehead that merged into a scalp. At one time he harbored thoughts of having a career. He would have made a good character actor, "the heavy" in gangster films, he thought. But that was before he decided to go behind the camera.

Burt had been more than an assistant director on the show. He was a "handler" who was paid by the producers to keep tabs on "the brat." Old habits die hard. Sometimes he was a bit heavy-handed, but the kid was impossible to control. Burt never did work again after the fire. The studio blamed him for provoking the kid. He lost his reputation and worse, his promised bonus. Had Burt known that he also would get cut out of the syndication earnings, he would have tracked Clay down that night and made him pay himself.

Standing up quickly, he leaned against the television stand, again feeling the effects from the altitude. He shut his eyes as the reporter continued interviewing the landlady.

"I didn't know who he was, but he owes me three months' rent."

"Do you have any indication where he went?" the reporter asked, pressing his microphone up to her face.

"He owes me three months' rent!"

Burt slammed the suitcase shut. He didn't know where Clay was, but he knew where he could find out, and she was going to tell him…or else. He left the motel room without bothering to turn off the television.

"Missing in action and outrunning the IRS. So where is 'Little Guy Mike'?"

Chapter Three

Clay slowly opened his eyes from the perfect night's sleep. The deep green eyes were the same, but the boy had faded — at least on the outside. He was thirty-three. His face masculine, his cheek bones and jaw defined. His hair, once dyed by the powers that be, was an unruly chestnut brown that covered his eyes when he sneezed.

His eyes focused on the persistent gleam of light coming from the pane-glassed window that looked out over the rugged harbor. "Room with a view" the ad read. It was the only window in the frugal salt box. And because it was set back, deep within the thick colonial wall, it was more like a porthole. Hey, it's a view, he thought, repositioning his head in the pillow.

He had been in Charlestown, Massachusetts three

months, almost the whole summer, and was finally sleeping through the night. For that, he was grateful. It always took him this long to settle into a new town. And just when he would start to feel at home, something would happen that would force him to move on. He would still be in Beaver Creek, Colorado had that ski instructor not recognized him. Did he have to ask out a former president of his fan club? This was always his dilemma: contort yourself to please others or stay true to you and be alone. For the past fifteen years, he chose the latter.

As a result, he had no one to talk to, really talk to. Writing was his only solace and now he was not even doing that. Words, he had discovered, only made him more aware of what he could never really change. And the voice that always comforted him, the one that he used to hear on the scaffolding, was now distant and faint.

Nestling his head in the pillow, he cherished these moments in bed, hidden beneath the protective summer blanket, feet tucked into the soft cotton sheet secured to the mattress.

I could spend eternity in here. He tried to ignore the fact that a coffin offered the same benefits.

Every year on his birthday, he did his best not to think about the night of the fire or the days that followed when he found himself in Costa Rica trying to disappear. Most runaways went to Hollywood. Clay ran everywhere else. South America, Thailand and then Europe, backpacking until the money ran out. It was nearly three years before he realized the studio covered up his involvement in the fire. He couldn't figure out why until he started seeing his face pop up on billboards and newsstands across Europe. The syndication was growing year by year. It didn't matter how obscure the town was.

He was in the Black Forest when he first learned about his troubles with the IRS. Clay didn't need to read German to know he wasn't responsible for a debt when he never saw a profit. Obviously, this was payback for covering up the fire.

Every place he went, "Little Guy Mike" followed. When he saw a child wearing a "Little Guy Mike" Halloween mask during Carnival, he knew it was time to go back. He was homesick and besides, because of the syndication, *Little Guy Mike* was more popular abroad than it had been in the States. That was five years ago.

He had been so many places, but because he kept to himself, each place felt the same.

His eyes gravitated to the only other source of light in the room, the blurry digital numbers of the alarm clock. They read 5:37 AM. "No!"

Clay emerged from bed as if an army officer had entered the barracks. Fumbling over his duffel bag in the darkness, he regained his balance for a teetering moment, and then succumbed to gravity, his 5'11" frame tumbling backwards onto the knotted pine floor. He seldom landed on his feet, but he did land.

Flat on his back, he stared upward, his eyes confirming that the low ceiling, like Heaven, always seemed higher from this vantage point. After a few moments, he pulled himself up, which he was also accustomed to doing.

As he rose, he saw her. This had become a morning ritual. Through that porthole of a window, he stared at her. The flapping colorful flags were draped over her elaborate rigging. The crew climbed her three proud masts, lowering her vast sails. Whatever majestic was, she was it. U.S.S. Constitution — Old Ironside… She made him want to be a better man. He knew that kind of inspiration was hard to come by.

His anxious eyes returned to the clock.

* * *

Boston is a walking town, but Clay was running.

Since the night of the fire he never had a good feeling about his birthday. He always thought something bad was going to happen. Usually it did.

The Washington Street Bridge connected Charlestown to the North End, crossing Boston Harbor where it met the Charles River. Sprinting across in record time, his frantic pace conjured up memories of being late to set. An unforgiving crew could make life miserable for a kid. It didn't matter if you were the star. The cold shoulder could last weeks. It was never his intention to be late, it was just his nature.

Traveling along the Freedom Trail, his swift feet followed the red brick line, darting past historical markers — churches, meeting houses, burying grounds —

that told the story of Boston's and the nation's struggle for freedom.

He appreciated that liberty was a precious thing and worth fighting for, but Clay wasn't interested in re-tracing his own Freedom Trail, that uneven road that began the night of the fire. As far as he was concerned, the people and events of his past were all best left in the past. He had paid a heavy price for walking away and did everything he could to ensure that it wasn't in vain.

Quickening his pace, he glanced up to align himself with the Old North Church's towering steeple. It was a constant beacon to ships entering the harbor. His on-set tutor made sure he knew the history. On the evening of April 18, 1775, Robert Newman climbed the belfry and held high two lanterns as a signal from Paul Revere that the British were marching to Lexington and Concord to arrest Samuel Adams and John Hancock and to seize the Colonial store of ammunition. That event ignited the American Revolution.

If warning lanterns were left this day, Clay could not tell as the rapidly emerging sun obscured his sight.

* * *

The Italian North End was already awake. Street vendors scattered empty produce crates among the stalls opening for the day, merchants arranged fresh fish in open containers filled with ice, while grandmothers hung laundry off tenement balconies.

Racing through the narrow walkways and alleys, he darted under a grand banner strung across the street.

92nd Annual Fisherman's Feast & Angel Flight
August 16-19
Music, Food and Fireworks

It had been a summer of feasts and this would be the largest. Clay avoided crowds, but knew a quiet existence would be possible once Labor Day passed. That was, if he still had a job.

He knew he got paid today, and after paying a few expenses, would finally have enough cash to send to his former landlady in Colorado.

Catching his breath, he arrived at 300 Hanover Street. The brown marquee read "Mike's Pastry" in stylized yellow lettering. It was a fixture in the immigrant neighborhood for over fifty years. It had occurred to him that "Little Guy Mike" working at Mike's Pastry was the equivalent of hiding in plain sight. So far the strategy had worked.

Clay went around back and cautiously poked his head in the door. He knew his best bet was to slip in once the manager was out of sight.

If Santa was Italian, this was what his workshop would look like — specialty cakes spinning on wheels as they were being decorated, trays of macaroons being removed from the stainless steel ovens, eggs added to dough churning in the industrial mixer. The aroma was invigorating. He loved this place.

The bakers were already loading pastry bags with ricotta cheese. They took a golden cannoli shell in one hand, then filled each side before dipping the ends in chocolate chips or mixed green nuts, dusting the top with confectioner's sugar.

He made eye contact with some of the bakers.

"Coast is clear," one of the bakers said. "He's in the front."

Stepping into the kitchen, he was careful to avoid Angelo De Spirito, the bakery's manager. "You guys are the best," he spoke softly. And they were. In the past three months he had yet to endure the cold shoulder. They didn't know who he was, but his quirky ways were a welcome distraction, as were his stories of Italy. As Clay was greeted by a host of first generation Italian bakers, he spotted Angelo approaching.

A baker intercepted Angelo by rolling a six-foot rack of empty cannoli shells in front of Clay. Another slid an apron over Clay's head, before the first baker spun the rack around. The guys always looked out for Clay. However, when Clay turned around he was face to face with Angelo.

"Again late," the stout manager reprimanded. "Everyone else 4:30. You 6:10!"

Clay nodded in agreement. He knew silence was his best bet.

"If the feast didn't start tonight…"

Clay continued to nod.

"Get to work!"

Clay smiled then got to work, moving the rack filled with cannoli. As soon as Angelo turned his back, he snuck one…tasted as good as it looked. Not a bad breakfast.

* * *

The North End readied for the feast — carnival games being assembled, policemen sectioning off streets, workers erecting a stage in the square, volunteers on ladders attaching green, white and red decorations to the lamp posts.

At Mike's Pastry, a line stretched out the door despite the hot and humid August weather. Among those toward the back of the line was a man with a Minolta slung over his shoulder. Casing his surroundings, Burt attempted to blend in with everyone else in line. Patience was not one of his virtues, but if the address was right, he wasn't about to blow the element of surprise.

Inside, the bakery was packed, bustling with a mixture of tourists and locals pressing up against the enormous glass case overflowing with a variety of authentic Italian pastry. Everything in this case was the real thing — pistachio nut macaroons, chocolate rainbows, lemon rings, chocolate Florentine, green leaves, apricot bows, fig squares. "Two pounds of the fancy macaroons!" one lady shouted, pointing to the glass case. "And a Lobster tail…with chocolate cream!" The activity was chaotic. Numbers were yelled out as workers anxiously filled white-and-blue boxes, before wrapping them in red-and-white string.

In the kitchen, the bakers intensified their pace, busy

keeping up with the demand while Clay was out back, assigned to a "special project" in the alley.

Clay unloaded bags of flour from the delivery truck, stopping momentarily to wipe the sweat from his forehead. The heat was oppressive, and he was obviously not happy.

"Next time on time," Angelo gloated before returning to the kitchen.

Clay offered a tortured stare, convinced Angelo was a studio boss in a former life. He hurled another bag off the truck.

Not long after, Angelo's ten-year-old daughter Bella appeared. She had the cherub face of an angel. Her naturally curly hair was auburn and competed with an adult-sized head that sat perfectly on her petite frame. Her sparkling brown eyes lit up as she smiled. She held two Italian ices, one in each hand.

"Lemon?" Clay shouted from the truck.

"Of course!"

Clay leaped off the truck overjoyed. Lemon was his favorite. Stumbling as he made his landing, he luckily regained his balance instead of falling over.

Bella exhaled, handing him the ice.

"You really are an angel," Clay confessed, wiping his brow. He held the cold ice up against his face. "I can see why they picked you over all the other girls."

"I don't want to be the angel," Bella pouted, twirling her curly locks with her finger.

"Why?" He rested on the bags of flour, devouring the

ice.

"The girl who's the angel has to hang from that!" Bella pointed to a rope on a pulley stretching across the street. It was three stories up, higher than the banner announcing the feast. "That's high!"

Wouldn't catch me up there, Clay thought to himself.

"All those people staring at me, I won't be able to remember the prayer." Bella paced, hands animated in the air.

Squeezing the last of his refreshing ice from the white paper cup, he glanced over and realized that Bella hadn't touched hers.

"They keep saying I'm lucky…lucky. But I don't want to do it!" She sat down discouraged, handing Clay her untouched ice. "I'm scared!"

Clay always did his best to numb his gift of empathy. Although it was the same quality that made him a good actor, it was a dangerous can of worms to open. It made him feel too deeply, sometimes for those who didn't deserve it. But what this little girl was feeling hit too close to home.

The ice in his hand quickly dissolved under the hot sun, but he didn't notice. Realizing how afraid she was, he turned his attention to the rope and pulley. In that moment, everything disappeared. It was as if he was dangling above the crowd, a boy again, forced to play the angel.

He was hanging there with that ridiculous baseball cap glued to his head, terrified and blinded by spotlights. People milled about beneath him, screaming his name. Brassy circus music filled the air.

"Where's my mom? Get me down! Somebody! Anybody!"

He could feel the ropes fraying.

"Listen to me! I don't like this!"

His desperate cries fell on deaf ears. He looked to the heavens.

"Aren't You going to help? Why should I keep talking to You if You're not going to help?

"I didn't choose this! I didn't choose this!" the boy cried.

Bella tugged on his shirt. "What is it?"

Clay came to himself, realizing that Bella was beside him. "You shouldn't have to do it if you don't want to. That's what I think. You're a little girl, not the entertainment."

"But if I don't have a choice, what can I do?"

Bella didn't have a choice, and nobody understood this better than Clay.

She placed her hands on the sides of her face and lowered her head, eyes staring hopelessly at the cobblestone pavement. "What can I do?"

If there was a time to be profound, this was it. At a loss for words, Clay took a moment to consider what he would do as a delivery truck passed by them in the alley.

"If it were me…," he turned to Bella, "I'd tell myself… I didn't choose this."

Bella nodded her head, agreeing. "I didn't choose this."

"But I'm up here…." Clay jumped up on the bags of flour to emphasize the point.

Bella raised her head in expectation.

"So…" Clay said, hesitating.

Bella hung on his every word. "So…?"

Clay stared at the pulley and rope, trying to complete his thought. "I might as well fly." Clay extended his arms, trying to sell the point.

"That's all you got?" Bella cried, dropping her head again.

"That's all I got," Clay said, jumping off the bags.

The little girl was distraught.

"Hey, don't worry. You're not going to be alone. I'm going to be there. If you don't like it, I'll make sure they bring you right down."

"You promise?"

Clay held up his hand. "I promise."

Angelo unexpectedly appeared from the kitchen, noticing the two speaking. "No breaks! No breaks!"

Clay grabbed a bag of flour in an attempt to look busy, but Angelo was focused on Bella.

"Go learn your prayer!" Angelo hollered.

Determined to get out of this honor, Bella stood abruptly and looked up at her father. "I don't want to do it!"

"What you mean?"

Bella quickly recognized the serious power imbalance and proceeded to climb atop the stack of bags. She was now eye level with her father.

"I'm a little girl, not the entertainment," she declared, pointing to the pulley and rope.

Angelo looked angrily at Clay who looked away.

"I'm serious, Papa. I'm not doing it."

Angelo slowly leaned forward, then fumed, "Go! Learn your prayer!"

Bella jumped off the bags and ran off discouraged.

Angelo turned to Clay. "You're fired!"

Inside the crowded bakery, Burt pushed his way to the front of the line. Pressed up against the glass case, Burt caught the attention of one of the ladies behind the counter. "Over here!"

"You need to take a number," she fired back.

"I'm looking for somebody. An old friend…." As the woman leaned over the counter, Burt spoke into her ear, describing Clay. Finally, the lady pointed out back.

Adrenaline raced through his body. After all this time, Clay was in range. Burt attempted to push his way through the crowd, but it was too thick. There was no way he was going to blow his chance. Glancing into the kitchen, he opted for a more direct path.

To the amazement of all in the bakery, Burt hopped the counter. Racing through the kitchen, the overweight photographer darted past the bakers with their trays of cannoli, and then out the back door toward Clay.

Clay untied his apron and was removing it over his head when he looked up and spotted Burt.

"No!"

Readying his camera, Burt charged at him.

"Happy Birthday…!"

Desperate, Clay reached for a bag of flour and using all his weight hurled it at Burt. As the bag made contact, the seams split open. Both crashed to the ground as a massive cloud of flour erupted followed by the bright flash of the camera.

Chapter Four

"Fact or Fake... Is this really Clay Grant, the elusive sitcom star seldom seen as an adult? 'Could be,' says one ENZ source that reports assault charges have been filed in Boston against this outlaw on the run."

If there was a name Ted Mitchell never needed to hear again it was Clay Grant. But like an accident on the freeway, he couldn't divert his eyes.

Ted walked toward the television in the hospital lobby, his eyes fixated on the photograph. It was of a guy amidst a cloud of flour. Only his eyes were partially visible.

"Over the years, ENZ has been inundated with hundreds of "Little Guy Mike" sightings from 40 states and 14 countries! Only problem is that no one is quite sure what the real LGM looks like."

Ted leaned in.

"Here is one of his last public appearances at the Orange Bowl in Miami."

Clay was joined on stage by inspirational pastor Reagan Mitchell and his teenage son.

Ted stared at a younger version of himself standing beside his father. It had been years since he had seen the clip. They had spent the summer touring stadiums with that anti-drug campaign and were half-way through when Clay was added to the line-up to help improve his public image. While Ted and his family actually cared about the message they shared, all too often Clay had been inches away from undermining everything. Thinking of it now still irked Ted.

"Boys what do you do when someone asks you to take drugs?"

Clay and Ted shouted, *"Just say no!"*

Smirking, Ted was surprised Clay stayed under the radar this long. *A guy like that creates a mess wherever he goes.* In Ted's opinion, Clay was everything Ted was not: reckless and impulsive and never concerned with making the right choice. The son of the pastor and always under the church's watchful eye, Ted had had to struggle to make straight A's and maintain his position on the varsity track team. He expected that good things came to those who worked hard for them, or at least that's what he had been taught. But life was telling him something different.

Moving down the hall, Ted continued his quest for Stanford University Hospital's late night version of dinner. So far he had mistakenly discovered the pharmacy, psychiatric ward and even the mortuary, but no vending machine. Dollar bill in hand, he was unwilling to admit that he might have been sent on a wild goose chase.

Just when he was about to give up, he turned the corner and spotted the machine inside a newly remodeled waiting room he had not yet discovered. This area was quieter than the one he had been sleeping in and boasted a new flat screen television.

Staring through the vending machine's glass, he searched for something healthy among the processed, fat-filled choices. Now his options were limited – Doritos, Pop Tarts, Corn Nuts. Despite being sleep deprived, he wasn't giving in. *A granola bar…. There we go.* Ted was fit and always tried to make the right choice when it came to eating and to life. This was his unspoken deal with God: choose wisely and nothing too bad will happen. To many, Ted's concern with his choices appeared emotionless, closed off. He knew what they said behind his back: Ted wasn't his father.

Feeding his dollar into the machine, it promptly spit it out. He flattened the dollar with this thumbs and fed it again. *Rejected!* Now he was annoyed, but still determined. Rubbing the dollar vigorously against the edge of the machine, he fed it once more. *Success!* Pressing E4 on the touchpad, Ted watched as the coils started to turn. *Come on, come on…* The granola bar inched forward as the coils continued their counterclockwise turn. His stomach growled...*come on.* Then, before his wide-eyes, the coils jammed, lodging the granola bar and leaving it dangling in midair.

Ted stared blankly through the glass, another right choice ending in frustration. Everything inside of him wanted to kick that machine, but as usual, he showed restraint. He tapped the glass a few times, but the granola bar didn't budge. Ted calmly looked to his right and to his left, and then, placing a hand on each side of the machine, he shook it violently. Huffing and puffing, he tried again, in vain.

"You need to push it from the front."

With hands still glued to the machine, he stopped and turned, realizing his nine-year-old son was standing beside him.

"I'm supposed to tell you that Mom called *again*... and that Grandpa wants Doritos."

"Tell grandpa the machine is broken..." Ted said calmly, hands still hugging the machine. "I'll see you back in the room." He watched his son walk away. He didn't want to admit it, but Ted secretly envied Clay's ability to get up and run at the first sign of trouble. He only wished he was capable of doing the same.

As the boy walked away, Ted banged his head in defeat against the machine. The granola bar dislodged from the coil, falling within reach. Ted looked at his own reflection in the glass. *Idiot....*

Retrieving the bar, he tore it open and began chewing his hard-fought prize. Ted crumpled the wrapper and, not spotting a trash can, reluctantly put it in his pocket before turning and walking away.

Chapter Five

Sounds from the first night of the feast filled the
Old North End Jail, fireworks bursting, an accordion
humming, people cheering. Beneath the iron-barred
window, still covered in flour, Clay sat defeated on the
cell's cold cement floor. He couldn't figure it out. How
did Burt keep finding him?

Over the years Clay had always managed to stay one
step ahead, but that was getting increasingly harder to do.

Clay hated admitting the power Burt had over him.
His presence was capable of making everything vanish,
the jail cell, the fifteen years, the man Clay believed he
had grown into. He was helpless again, his tormentor
within range. Clay wanted to get up and run away,
believing that would make the feelings dissipate, but he
was forced to sit there.

Pressing his hands against his ears, he leaned back against the crude brick wall. In this moment, he realized how much he hated the sound of a massive crowd, the imposing mixture of screams and laughter that violated his being. All he ever wanted was not to feel this again.

Looking up, he saw the guard approach the cell. He was holding a towel.

"Here." The guard tossed it through the bars.

Reaching for the towel, he wiped his face, but the flour was caked on. He could taste it. It was in his ears, his nostrils, his eyelashes and other places he didn't want to be reminded of. Each time he mistakenly touched his hair, a puff of flour rose into the air. Pulling himself up, he went to the exposed porcelain sink. Turning on the rusty faucet, he wet the towel. He scrubbed but struggled to get it off.

"You look like a ghost," the guard observed, peering through the bars.

Staring at himself in the mirror, Clay did not see a face, only the reality of all that had led up to this moment: the series of events, the choices and decisions, fifteen years running. *How did I let this happen?* Here he was again, trapped, ready to be exploited. Through the caked-on flour, he saw only fragments of the man he thought he had become. Everything was in jeopardy now. He knew the media would be descending on Boston soon. He wet the towel again.

Sightings of Clay were akin to the Loch Ness Monster. It always took a few days for the story to go from the rumor mill to the mainstream press. He had to get out before then.

Outside, a rock band began playing. The jubilant noise grew louder, sounds of song, cheers and laughter merging into one unpredictable reverberation.

Clay turned on both faucets, but the rushing water did little to drown out the noise. He scrubbed more vigorously, as if he was sanding his own skin, doing his best to focus in on any other sound than what was coming through that window.

"You're lucky to be in here," the guard shouted, "Two more nights of this! Crazy Italians…!"

Clay did not respond. With eyes focused on the mirror, he continued scrubbing away.

"You're not Italian?" the guard said, realizing his own political incorrectness.

Clay shook his head, no.

The guard continued to make casual conversation as he moved closer to the cell bars. He had a purpose. He was trying to see Clay's reflection in the mirror. "You know the last night they actually dress a little girl as an angel and hang her from a rope…three stories up. Crazy I tell you."

Clay thought of Bella as he splashed water on his face. He should have told her the truth. *There's nothing you can do.*

As Clay wiped the water from his face, the guard spotted a partial view of his clean reflection.

"You're him, aren't you?" The guard was excited, but still unsure.

Clay did not flinch. He just stared into the mirror.

"You're in a lot of trouble. Are you sure you don't want to call someone?

Clay remained silent, running his fingers through his wet hair.

As the guard turned to leave, Clay stared into the mirror and finally spoke. "Could you get me some paper? Some paper and a pen…?"

Puzzled, the guard nodded, yes.

* * *

The festivities from the first night of the feast died out around 1 AM, but Clay had just started scribbling. He sat on the cement floor, the pages clasped in his hand as he wrote. It was finally still enough for him to listen, if not to God's voice, his own. It was the only thing he could do. It was the only thing he knew how to do. Clay hadn't written in years, and for a moment, wondered if he could, but what he wrote had played out in his mind a thousand times before.

He didn't know exactly what he was writing, a defense, a eulogy, a document to remind himself that he wasn't who they said he was. Everyone else would have their say tomorrow, but this was his.

Clay fell asleep on the floor, leaning up against the brick wall.

A few hours later he was awoken by the guard.

"You're going to the courthouse."

Clay wiped the sleep out of his eyes.

Gathering the three pages he had written, he stuffed them in his back pocket before standing. He wouldn't be alone. This would be with him.

He went to the sink, splashed some water on his face and ran his fingers through his hair before turning to leave.

The holding room at the courthouse was only slightly larger than the jail cell but without windows. The arraignment was set to begin within the hour, but Clay's court-appointed lawyer had yet to show.

Pacing the room, he thought about representing himself, but knew he didn't have credibility in the court's eyes. He had been defending himself for as long as he could remember. He had been on trial his whole life, at the studio and in the court of public opinion. *But this was all too sick.* After all these years, after everything he did to ensure his freedom, Burt had him cornered.

Clay's lawyer was on the phone when he finally arrived, shaking Clay's hand with a firm grip, but waiting until he was finished with the call before giving him his full attention.

"Don't worry. I've reviewed the case. I got this all under control," Spaulding said smiling. His cell rang again. "Oh sorry, this is important. Just one minute…."

Clay shook his head.

Once Spaulding was off his cell, he explained his strategy. He was convinced that once it was revealed that Burt had worked on the show, the case would be dismissed. Clay was not so sure.

"This is a slam dunk!" Spaulding assured him.

Clay hated the idea that he was in the hands of another person. He thought Jeffery Spaulding looked the part of a lawyer, but lacked the believability to persuade a judge. This guy was boisterous with an overconfidence that made Clay uneasy.

"Judges don't like me. They want to make examples of guys like me, and, besides, you don't know Burt!

They argued back and forth, Spaulding discrediting most of what Clay said. Clay needed to hear Spaulding's "Plan B," but it was clear he didn't have one.

The bailiff opened the door. "Show time…."

Frustrated, Clay finally pulled out the pages he had written and circled one section before handing it to him.

"Use this…."

Spaulding glanced at it with a patronizing stare.

To appease Clay, Spaulding refolded the pages and stuffed them into his suit pocket. "I've been doing this awhile," he assured him. "Trust me."

Clay felt the familiar panic as they walked through the door. Hearing "trust me" from a lawyer *never* ended well.

Chapter Six

The steady hum of oscillating fans filled the historic courtroom, drowning out the lawyers arguing before the judge during the arraignment. The air conditioning was down again, and the fans were another short-term solution to an ongoing problem. It didn't help that the brick courtroom was on the third floor or that the Federal-style windows were bare, ran floor to ceiling and faced the noon-day sun. So on days like this, the emboldened sun poured in uninhibited by anything except the judge herself. It was obvious she was sweltering beneath her black robe with the intense heat at her back. The golden laser beams braised her shoulder before traveling across the bench and landing into the courtroom.

This hour the sharp rays took aim at Clay. The sun

blazed against his face as the judge addressed the prosecutor.

"Why is Mr. Cummings wearing a neck brace?"

"He injured his neck in the fall, Your Honor."

Clay shifted uncomfortably in his seat.

Spaulding was quick to explain. "Burt Cummings charged at my client while he was unloading a truck at his place of employment."

"He hit him with a forty-pound bag of flour —"

"Self-defense —"

"With a forty-pound bag of flour?"

Burt was in his glory; he had Clay exactly where he wanted him. Clay had robbed him of his livelihood, his reputation and his share of the earnings. He had gotten away with the fire and so much more, but not this. Finally, he would pay. Finally, someone else would see Clay for what he really was....

"Many celebrities feel like assaulting the press, but they don't because of something called The First Amendment."

Clay looked at his lawyer. Spaulding spoke up. "Mr. Cummings isn't just a member of the press. He previously worked on *Little Guy Mike*...."

The judge glanced directly at Burt.

"He made a living on my client's childhood and is now stalking him...."

"Oh, please," the prosecutor was annoyed.

"Yes stalking him in a further effort to exploit his celebrity for monetary gain."

Burt hoped the court didn't know he released that picture of Clay covered in flour, but it was a quick buck, and besides no one could make his face out.

"He was taking his picture. How is that a crime?"

Clay leaned over and whispered in his lawyer's ear, but his lawyer subtly motioned him to be quiet.

The prosecutor wouldn't let up. "Burt Cummings may have previously worked on the show, but he is currently a member of the press. It is still legal to take a celebrity's picture."

The judge nodded in agreement.

Clay knew he was in trouble.

The arraignment was underway when Reagan Mitchell stepped into the courtroom; his noble stature and steel blue eyes were softened by his endearing smile. It was a closed court, but the seventy-one-year-old inspirational pastor had a national reputation; he could motivate anyone to do just about anything. The vitality in his voice and his sturdy presence always inspired confidence. A person's shortcomings, he believed, were always problems solved with a new vision. His books were roadmaps to a better life. Lately, he questioned his own sense of direction. Reagan knew leaving Cliff Falls now would cause friction at home, but he had a clear motive for making the cross-country journey.

Ascending the staircase, Reagan took a seat in the balcony without being noticed. Peering down at the action below, he quickly became concerned.

The judge opened Clay's case history, reviewing it aloud. "June 'ninety-seven, creating a public disturbance,

August 'ninety-seven, destruction of public property…"

"He was trying to get out of dodge, Your Honor. He was being chased by paparazzi…"

"May 'ninety-eight, mayhem, reckless driving…"

"Similar circumstances, Your Honor…"

"February 'ninety-nine, mayhem, destruction of private property, reckless driving… Mr. Spaulding, how many names does your client go by?"

"My client has routinely used alternate names to protect his anonymity. It's perfectly legal…."

The prosecutor interrupted. "He also has a habit of skipping out on landlords…."

The judge stared at Clay over her glasses. "You're *really* that little guy?" she said sarcastically.

Clay smirked at her, embarrassed.

"My client has made restitution. If you look in his file, you'll see…."

"There is always an explanation. It's always someone else's fault," the prosecutor said. "Personal responsibility," the prosecutor added glancing at Clay. "That's what separates Ron Howard from Danny Bonaduce. Personal responsibility…."

The judge nodded in agreement.

Reagan knew no one could argue with that. He wanted to descend the staircase and represent Clay himself. He was not a lawyer, but was capable of doing what the law could never do: persuade a crowd.

Spaulding looked lost.

The courtroom was silent except for the steady hum

of the fans that resembled static on a broadcast that had been unexpectedly interrupted.

The sun's rays were now directed at Spaulding who looked defeated. He tugged at his tie as the heat began to affect him, the noticeable perspiration beading upon his forehead.

"Anything else?" the judge asked.

Clay cleared his throat to get his lawyer's attention. With subtle glances and stares they argued back and forth. Finally, against his better judgment, Spaulding reluctantly reached into his suit pocket and removed the folded pages.

"Anything else?" the judge repeated.

"If I may…" he said to the judge as he unfolded the pages. Spaulding glanced at what Clay had circled and then read a few lines.

"Clay is a screw up. We're not going to argue that. If that's what you're looking for there's plenty to find.

"We think of child stars as cute dolls created for our entertainment. Then we judge them mercilessly when they grow up and stumble, all the while thinking of them as the collective property of those they once entertained.

"Clay is not a doll. He is not a meal ticket. He is a human being." Spaulding had life in his eyes, a passion that had been missing.

Reagan smiled with confidence. Finally, Spaulding was humanizing Clay.

"My client is not a sympathetic figure. Look at his file," Spaulding conceded.

"The faxes are still coming in," the judge said, indicating the thick file.

"It's all a desperate attempt to reclaim his life," Spaulding said. "He's done everything he can do to live a quiet, normal life. It's time we left him alone." He pointed to Burt. "What about this man's choices? How long can someone be hunted without protection from the court?"

Spaulding was on a roll, and he knew it. "What would they find if they dug up Mr. Cummings' past, or mine, or any of us here today in this courtroom? I guarantee you that if they looked hard enough, they'd find what they were looking for...and plenty more."

He glanced at the page again and looked up, adding his own words. "I humbly ask the court, the prosecution, Mr. Cummings...when you look at Clay, 'what are you looking for?' because that's what you're going to find."

"Nice sentiment, Spaulding," the judge said. "I didn't know you had it in you."

Sensing some empathy, Clay looked at the judge hoping that she saw him as something more than a commodity.

The judge continued. "I can assure Mr. Grant that this court does not view you as pop culture property."

Clay and his lawyer glanced at each other.

"Motion to dismiss granted. Further I am granting the restraining order requested against Mr. Cummings."

Clay exhaled.

Spaulding triumphantly clenched the crumpled paper.

"However," the judge added, "Mr. Grant is not free to go. The federal government is not as sympathetic as this court."

The judge removed a document from the file and held it up. "Unfortunately, in your absence your estate neglected to pay the IRS on your syndication earnings. You are responsible for $478,000 in back taxes."

Clay whispered into Spaulding's ear.

"My client's estate squandered those earnings," Spaulding pleaded. "He never saw a dime of that money."

"Regardless, the law is clear. I cannot give Mr. Grant another opportunity to run. Bail is set at $100,000." The gavel fell.

Clay was crushed. There was nothing he could do.

Reagan rose to his feet and exited the balcony.

"It's about time you learned this lesson," the judge stared at Clay over her glasses. "Running never makes it better."

The bailiff removed Clay from the courtroom. As Clay was led out, he could feel Burt glaring at him. Clay knew this wasn't over. Burt wasn't finished with him yet.

Reagan, now on the court floor, watched as Spaulding crumpled up the paper and lobbed it into the trash. As the judge stepped down from the bench, Reagan approached her, holding a hardback book entitled, *The Road to Hope.*

"This is a closed court. How did you get in here?" the judge asked, looking at him suspiciously.

"Your honor, I'm Reagan Mitchell." In hopes of establishing credibility, Reagan pointed to his own picture on the back of his book.

"You're that guy?"

"I'm that guy."

As the judge took her last step off the bench, the unforgiving light at her back filled the courtroom. The sharp rays now took aim at Reagan, shining directly into his confident face. "May I have a moment?"

Chapter Seven

Clay peered through the cell's iron-barred window as the feast continued, his eyes watching the slow moving processional. The crowd cheered as they marched behind the revered statue of the Madonna and Little King.

The Little King sat on his mother's lap beneath an ornate canopy of gilded azure cloth on a platform the men were careful to keep steady. It was as if she were protecting him. The Little King was donned in a jeweled crown and a flowing robe woven with gold thread and covered in dollar bills pinned to the cloth. Clay thought the robe looked heavy. As the relic was paraded down the street, Clay identified with the Little King, staring into his empathetic eyes, eyes that looked deeply into him.

The sound of the crowd transported him back to his youth. *He was waving to a cheering audience at the conclusion of a taping. As he removed his signature baseball cap the audience roared. He tossed it into the crowd, creating pandemonium as the people fought over the hat. People were always trying to get a piece of him.*

As Clay walked off set, a callous hand grabbed his arm and shook him violently, pinning him up against the wall. Clay caught his breath in fear, tightening his gut, his shoulder throbbing where it had been dislocated before.

Clay's memory was abruptly interrupted when the guard entered.

"You have a visitor."

Clay began to panic as he faced the window, hands pressed against the brick wall. "I said no cameras, no visitors."

"This one posted your bail," the guard shot back, sorting through the key ring.

Slowly, Clay turned from the window, and then saw Reagan Mitchell standing beside the guard. Clay was bewildered.

"It's been a long time," Reagan smiled warmly.

The guard held up the key, waiting for his response. Clay nodded, and the guard unlocked the gate.

Reagan stepped into the cell as the guard locked the gate behind him before leaving. He cautiously engaged Clay, who was silent. "I think the last time I saw you, you were, what, sixteen?"

Reagan took a moment, searching for the boy within the man standing before him. He couldn't get over how different he looked. "If it wasn't for those eyes, I don't think I could recognize you."

Clay lowered his gaze.

Reagan tried another direction, moving around the cell, avoiding direct eye contact. "That was some argument your lawyer made, 'People find what they're looking for' — a very effective line."

"Seventeen — I was seventeen."

"Yes…seventeen. We must have toured a dozen stadiums that summer. 'Just Say No.' If only life were that simple." Reagan sat on the edge of the mattress feeling the springs of the metal bed.

Clay faced the window, peering out. "Wasn't your son on that tour?"

"Yes." Reagan proceeded, feeling he gained a measure of trust from Clay. "Ted's a pastor now at our church in Cliff Falls."

"I already believe in the Good Book, if that's why you're here?" Clay said defensively. He never had a hard time believing in the existence of God, but they weren't exactly on speaking terms. "Try my stalker. I'm sure he can help you meet your quota."

"I flew 3,000 miles to remind you that you matter." Reagan rose to his feet. "Whatever trouble you are in, I am here to help."

Clay looked directly into Reagan's eyes. "What do you want?"

"In a way I feel responsible. I saw the pressure you were under. You were only a boy. I should have done something. Some adult should have done something."

"And you think you can do something now?"

"I'd like to try. It's been too long, but by the looks of things, nothing's gotten better...."

Clay had only known the confident Reagan, but now as Clay looked at him he saw something different, a frailty in his eyes. Maybe he was sick, maybe he was getting old, but Clay couldn't ignore his sincerity.

"I can't just sit by and watch another young life wasted, especially one with so much potential."

Clay pointed to the jail bars. "Potential is not exactly my top priority right now."

"I want to help you escape all of this, if you'll let me." Reagan put his hand on Clay's shoulder. He felt Clay flinch in a knee-jerk reaction.

Embarrassed, Clay squeezed the bars, staring blankly out of the cell. "How do you escape a life that lives in syndication?"

"Do you know what you want?" Reagan realized that it was a loaded question.

"What do I want...?" The truth was Clay only knew what he didn't want, but decided to indulge the man. "You know that old ship in the harbor?"

"Old Ironside...?"

"I want to hijack her...take her out of the harbor and find some place I can be left alone. Some place I can find peace."

"Can you envision such a place?"

Clay closed his eyes and painted a picture of a place he had obviously dreamed of.

"It would have to have a lot of trees—kind of a mountainous place...like Colorado. Somewhere I could exhale."

"What else?" Reagan leaned forward, coaxing him on.

"Well, it couldn't be too far from the water. I'd need to know if things ever got really bad, I could jump on a ship and sail away."

"Anything else...?"

Clay opened his eyes. "How could I forget? There would be *no television*!"

Reagan laughed at the unrealistic request.

"Or at least very bad reception..."

"So there is only one question left: If you knew such a place actually existed, would you have the courage to go there?"

Clay now shifted uncomfortably.

"I spoke with the judge. She's agreed to release you into my custody."

"The judge agreed to that?"

"There are conditions. I would pay a third of your debt to the IRS up front."

"You'd do that?" Clay said with disbelief.

Reagan nodded.

"What else?" Clay said looking for the catch.

"I would provide you with a job to pay off the rest and make a series of reports to the court."

"Doing what exactly?"

Reagan smiled warmly. "I'll come up with something."

"I don't know."

"Believe it or not, you just described Cliff Falls right

down to the lousy television reception. It's tucked in the Santa Cruz Mountains of Northern California, fifteen minutes from the ocean. It's beautiful. Trees, hiking trails, plenty of space to breathe."

"I'm desperate, but a church?" He was only partially sorry for the insult.

"You could avoid the media circus."

"I don't know."

"I have to get back. I've been away too long as it is. You will be released later tonight. That should give you time to slip out before anyone realizes you're gone." Reagan pulled a business card out of his wallet and handed him a few hundred dollars, "It's probably not smart to go back to your apartment."

Clay held the money in his hand. "You trust me?"

"There will be a ticket waiting for you at the airport tomorrow."

"You're betting on the wrong horse. Google me…I'm famous for letting people down."

"Funny thing about Old Ironside is that it's made of wood…oak from the Carolina swamp." Reagan motioned for the guard who unlocked the gate. "The Brits bombarded that ship with sixteen-pound cannon balls. And you know what? They ricocheted off. The young sailors couldn't believe their eyes when they saw that the cannon balls were simply bouncing off its hull."

The guard shut the gate.

Reagan glanced through the bars. "Who knew wood could be so strong?"

* * *

Clay was released in the early morning hours. The North End was still except for the sweeper truck that drove past him clearing the road of trash from the feast the night before. For the moment he was safe.

He paused on the corner, checking his pocket for the cash Reagan gave him. *What was this guy up to?* What made Reagan think he wouldn't take the money and run? This time nobody would find him.

Further down the street, Clay noticed the rope and pulley in the town square. He couldn't help but think of Bella, wondering if she would be all right. He had made a promise to her. Someone had to reassure the little girl that she could do it…that those ropes would hold her.

Clay watched as the first news van set to cover the Angel Flight pulled into the North End. Pulling his beige knit hat lower, he moved on.

Chapter Eight

Documents flapped beneath paperweights as the 1960's metal fan blasted the counter in the clerk's office before rotating and refreshing the line of people seated in the waiting area. The ancient fan with woven cord was a fire hazard justified as another short-term solution.

In the back office, a distracted jail clerk held a hundred-dollar bill in his hand as Burt struggled in vain to find information of Clay's release.

"That's all I know," the clerk insisted, shuffling through his files.

"Who posted his bail?" Burt pressed, waving two more Ben Franklins. He had cash on hand from a few small-time paparazzi jobs, and didn't mind dolling it out in hopes of a bigger return. He knew the rest of the media would be showing up soon.

"It was a 'special arrangement of the court.' Only the judge knows."

"You're telling me no one, except for the judge, knows where he is?"

"He won't be in hiding for long." The clerk reached into a file, and then held up Clay's mug shot, waving it tauntingly at Burt. "Not after this is released. Of course that would make any photo you take worthless," the clerk smirked, fanning himself with the mug shot.

Burt knew the guy was bluffing. "This district doesn't release mug shots to the public. I already checked."

"Not officially, but these shots do have a way of getting leaked to the press," the clerk smirked again.

"I'll give you a grand to lose that photo."

Chapter Nine

The Fisherman's Feast and Angel Flight banner was illuminated with strings of glowing lights. Below, a brass band played as the massive crowd filled the narrow streets and sidewalks in anticipation of the grand finale. Since 1911, the soaring pronouncement was the same: the young angel's petition to the Madonna for the Fishermen's safe return home from sea.

Bella peered out the third story window practicing her Italian prayer, her angelic voice trembling as she repeated each line. Word had gotten out about Clay's release. She just knew he was there somewhere, but couldn't spot him among the faces in the crowd.

"All these people came to see you," Bella's grandmother said, placing the gold crown on her curly locks. She pressed it down, securing it with Bobbie pins.

"It's too tight!" Bella said squinting.

Her grandmother was unmoved. "Smile Bella…smile!"

Bella glanced out the window, forcing a nervous smile.

"In just a few moments one lucky girl will make the traditional flight on this the last night of the Fisherman's Feast," the reporter said into the camera. "I am now standing with Angelo De Spirito who is not only the father of this year's angel, but the manager of this landmark bakery. Did you have any idea 'Little Guy Mike' was working in your bakery?"

"I only watch *M*A*S*H* and *Who's the Boss?*" If Tony Danza worked in my bakery, I'd know it."

"Do you have any indication where he went?" the reporter pressed. "Has he tried to make contact with you or your daughter?"

Angelo shrugged his shoulders.

Burt was milling about in the crowd, having ditched his neck brace hours ago. His camera was tucked on the inside of his jacket. He wasn't about to let a restraining order stop him. He got a tip on how close Clay was to the little girl playing the angel and wouldn't put it past him to show up.

Bella sat on the window sill with her back to the crowd, gripping her fragrant bouquet. Men on the fire escape attached the wooden pulley to the harness hidden beneath her flowing blue-and-white gown while ropes were tied to her legs to help maintain her body position once in the air.

This was the moment. Bella clenched her eyes as she was yanked out the window, her outstretched arms shaking as she was hoisted above the masses. Despite the shouts and cheers of the crowd, she could still hear her grandmother's voice.

"They all came to see you, Bella! Smile for the people …smile!"

She forced a smile, but refused to open her eyes. Hovering above the crowd, ropes tied to her legs steadied her into position. She knew it was time.

Bella unclenched her eyes, but was quickly overwhelmed by the hundreds of blurry faces surrounding her. They were everywhere, in the streets, on the rooftops, peering out their apartment windows. Her throat tightened, her body trembling with fear. She searched the faces, but couldn't find Clay anywhere.

They lowered her to the Madonna and child to begin the prayer. The canopied statue was covered in dollar bills pinned to the flowing ribbons.

"The prayer Bella, the prayer…!" Angelo shouted.

She could hear her father's voice, but it didn't matter. Although she had practiced it a thousand times before, she could not remember it. Perhaps it was the sight of the crowd or possibly that she had been praying another prayer—a desperate plea for help and courage—as she was yanked out the window. It was a prayer without words, but one that was stronger than any she had prayed before. It was so real, that now a prayer with words was as foreign to her as flying above the crowd. She stared at the Madonna and child pleading for help, but she could not remember the proclamation.

"It seems our angel has forgotten her prayer," the reporter said into the camera. The scores of people waited for the prophetic pronouncement. You could hear a pin drop.

"Say something, Bella! Say something…anything!" Angelo cried with embarrassment.

Finally, Bella spoke. "I didn't choose this!" she said dangling above the multitude.

The crowd had a collective look of confusion.

"I didn't…" Bella prayed for courage. "But I'm up here. So…"

The crowd hung on her every word, waiting for her to finish the sentiment.

"…I might as well fly!"

Bella nodded to the men holding the rope. Within moments she began to move, flying back and forth, finally soaring over the crowd. "I might as well fly!"

The spectators cheered as she picked up speed, soaring over the narrow streets, the wind blowing against her face. "I might as well fly!"

People on the rooftops threw shreds of white paper onto the crowd, filling the sky and covering the street.

"Out of the mouths of babes," the reporter said into the camera. "Quite a turn of events in the North End…a new prayer at the Angel Flight, and a confirmation that 'Little Guy Mike' was indeed working at Mike's Pastry… unbelievable. I guess the only question left is, 'Where is Little Guy Mike'?"

Across the way in an empty building, a man in sunglasses and a beige knit hat watched from the rooftop. As the crowd dispersed, Burt looked up and spotted him. *Yes.…*

Pushing his way through the crowd, he darted into the building. Burt raced up the steps, positioning his camera. He had blown the element of surprise at the bakery. He wouldn't make the same mistake twice. Bursting through the door, the man's back was just in front of him. The perfect picture was just a tap on the shoulder away.

Readying his camera with one hand, he reached out with the other.…

Chapter Ten

Clay felt a hand on his shoulder as he was awakened by a flight attendant.

"Sir, your seat. You need to bring it back up."

Squinting at her below the rim of his beige knit hat, he nodded. As Clay raised his seat, his eyes slowly glanced around the cabin. It killed him to break his promise to Bella, but they each had their own flight to make this night.

Clay had to get out while he could. The media would be there and probably Burt. He had risked sneaking back to his apartment to gather what would fit in his duffel bag and backpack. It wasn't a lot, just a few essentials. Once again, he had to leave most of what he had behind. He was lucky to fly out of Manchester, NH, instead of Boston's Logan, which Burt would surely scout.

Clay felt the rumble of the landing gear beneath his feet.

"This is the captain. We have begun our decent into SFO. The temperature is a cool 57 degrees. We should be on the ground in twenty minutes."

Clay turned his attention out the oval window, the illuminated skyline emerging through pockets of the thick clouds. He focused on the city landscape below. He was searching for the place Reagan described. *I don't see any mountains.*

The taxi circled the remainder of the airport before merging onto the freeway onramp. As the taxi banked south onto Highway 101, Clay spotted a red wall of glowing brake lights. "Traffic always this bad?"

"You should have seen it during the technology boom," the cabbie said in the rear-view mirror. "Back then even I worked at a start up."

Clay cracked the window open. The smell of exhaust filled his nostrils. Plenty of room to breathe...? With eyes fixed on the traffic, he was doubtful. *Cliff Falls is probably an office complex on top of Knob Hill.*

"Hold on," the cabbie shouted, maneuvering onto the breakdown lane. Clay heeded his advice, grabbing the door railing. The taxi picked up speed as it headed west, accelerating down the expressway.

The cabbie pointed beyond the dash. "That's where we're going."

Clay glanced up, leaning forward in amazement. Straight ahead, through the cab's front window, he spotted a mountain range in the distance. *Maybe Reagan was telling the truth?*

The taxi skimmed past a sign that read "Highway 280," the highway opened up revealing a series of majestic mountains glowing in the deep purple and orange hues of sunset.

"They call this the most beautiful highway in the world."

Clay was quickly mesmerized by the vast mountainous landscape draped with a blanket of sturdy trees lining the rugged ridges. He rolled down the window the rest of the way and felt the vigorous breeze against his face.

Accelerating past vast fields of horses and cattle before climbing upward, the taxi wound through the narrow mountain road, ascending with the towering redwoods and oaks. Clay felt invigorated by the fresh forest air. *Could this really be a new beginning?*

Passing a carved wooden marker that read "Welcome to Cliff Falls," Clay took in the surroundings of the quaint town as the taxi traveled down the main street. It was pocketed with rustic, ranch-style establishments peeking through the foliage. *Walnut Grove meets Mayberry?* But he also knew looks could be deceiving. The town was so appealing that it could have been built on a studio backlot. Clay half wondered if real businesses were behind those storefronts or if the streets ended abruptly once they curved out of sight.

"Where in Cliff Falls?" the cabbie asked, reducing his speed.

"A church…High Hope Community," Clay pulled out

a business card, but the cabbie knew where it was.

"I don't care what they say," the cabbie commented in the rear-view mirror. "I think that Reagan is a good guy."

Clay sat puzzled as the taxi made its way toward the church. Driving up along Ridge Road, the church sign was just up ahead.

High Hope Community Church
A Family for You!

For a moment he allowed himself to imagine really having a family, but he knew better than to put stock in a tagline. He had made that mistake before. Pulling into the driveway, the headlights illuminated the crowded parking lot.

"What's going on here tonight?" the cabbie said.

Clay glanced out the window. Despite all the cars, no one was in sight. Where was everybody?

"You can let me out here," Clay said with a breath of caution. The tires eased to a stop. Paying the cabbie, he stepped out of the taxi onto the gravel pavement.

"It's up there," the cabbie said pointing to an illuminated cross at the top of the hill.

"Wait here," Clay said with a hesitation, putting on his backpack. If things went south, he wanted a clean escape. He was miles from civilization, on top of a mountain range and knew he wouldn't be able to make his way back now that it was dark.

"I've got to get back to the city—"

"Just a few minutes," Clay insisted, tightening the straps on his backpack. Shutting the door, he made his way past the double parked cars onto a path at the base of the steep hill.

Walking upward along the curving pathway, he passed thick oaks and redwoods as he made his way toward the front of the church. He listened to the leaves flapping, wind rustling through the trees.

He told himself not to overreact because of all the cars, that it was probably BINGO night. He took several more steps and then stopped. "Wait, only Catholics play BINGO."

Moving further up the hill, he focused on the white steeple—a vague reminder of the Old North Church — and an illuminated cross peeking out above the trees. It was the only light save the craftsman-style lanterns that lined the path. Gripping his duffel bag, Clay did his best to ignore the uneasy sense of foreboding as deadened leaves crunched beneath his feet.

He told himself that it wasn't too late to turn back. But the truth was he could never go back. That was one lesson he learned early on. He had been so many places over these fifteen years, but back was never one of them.

As he neared the crest, he spotted the end of the path and then strangely, a brilliant light glaring in the distance. Surrounded by darkness, he cautiously walked into the light as if he was having a near death experience. Moving forward, he struggled to make out what lay on the other side of the light. Forcing his pupils to focus, the reality suddenly came into view.

In the glow of the clapboard church he spotted a row of news vans with satellite dishes mounted on top. Blurry eyes strained, he watched media crews setting up shots: cameramen with equipment resting on their shoulders awaited the signal while reporters with microphones in hand prepared for the live remote. Clenching his duffel bag, Clay realized that this reception was for him.

"He didn't!" he said, panicking.

Turning away from the light, he looked back down the hill, but the taxi was gone. He struggled to catch his breath. Desperate, he took cover behind a protective oak tree, his heart racing as he leaned back against the coarse bark.

Peering around the tree, his eyes stared directly into the manufactured light. "You son of a bitch. You set me up!"

Chapter Eleven

Pressing his face against the bark, Clay peeked around the oak at the hungry media, staring at his reward for trusting Reagan. *A step of faith right into a ditch!*

"That's not a very good hiding place," a boy said, wheezing.

Turning abruptly, Clay's cheek scraped as it pulled away from the bark. Looking down, he realized the boy, maybe nine-years-old, was standing beside him.

Wheezing, the boy stared at Clay through a blond mop top that had obviously been styled with a wet comb. Dressed like a miniature accountant, he wore a crisp white shirt and navy striped tie. Gasping for air, he searched the contents of his khaki's left pocket: a pack of bubble gum, a hand held video game and a few baseball cards.

"Excuse me?" Clay said, ducking back behind the tree.

Reaching into the other pocket he finally removed an asthma inhaler. Giving it a good shake, he gave himself a solid burst of air. "I said…" the boy spoke slowly, emphasizing his point, "that's not a very good hiding place."

"Who said I'm hiding?" Clay shot back, careful to keep his voice down so as not to draw attention.

"The church balcony is your best bet," the boy glanced over his shoulder, pointing at the church, "but don't stay there too long 'cause after a while they come looking for you there, too."

The kid was wise beyond his years. Clay turned his head towards the church. In front of him a media circus ready to exploit him, behind him this kid who had seen right through him. Clay's despair was interrupted by the rustling of dead leaves at his back. He turned immediately.

The boy now resembled a determined, but misdirected Houdini. Spinning in the dirt, he frantically tugged at his diminished, but stronger knot in his tie. The harder he pulled, the tighter the knot became.

"Easy!" Clay said, dropping his duffel bag to the ground. Fearing the boy might choke himself Clay offered to help him with the knot. He was careful to ask first, something adults rarely did when he was a kid.

The boy nodded repeatedly, his grateful blue eyes seemingly dilated.

"Relax," Clay said as he worked the knot. "The secret is to relax."

The boy rolled his eyes, obviously incapable of relaxing while constrained in this formal garb.

Clay reluctantly smiled. *Point well taken.* "Ever heard of a clip-on?" he said, as the tips of his fingers separated the twisted tie. "You know if you lose this they can't make you wear it." Clay thought a kid should know his options.

As the tie came undone, the boy exhaled, letting out a loud gasp. "I can breathe! I can breathe!" He stood up dizzily, un-tucking his shirt, inhaling the night air. But the celebration would be short-lived.

"Tyler!" a woman's voice hollered in the distance.

The boy's eyes widened.

"Tyler!" the voice screamed louder.

Clay watched as Tyler gasped for air.

"Here!" the boy whispered, handing Clay his tie. Reaching down, he grabbed his baseball cards, bubble gum and video game before running off in the opposite direction from where the voice cried. Catching his breath he added, "You never saw me!"

Hastily sliding back behind the tree, Clay watched the boy veer down a trail and disappear into the darkness. He was envious, recalling a time when he could disappear that fast. Clay looked at the navy striped tie in his hand. Searching for a place to hide it, he finally stuffed it in his back pocket. Inching his body around the perimeter of the tree, the woman passed on the other side on her way down the hill.

Pressed up against the bark, he looked at the reporters wondering if Burt was among them. He knew the media would be headed his way, and the kid was right, this tree wasn't going to conceal him all night.

Clay deliberately banged his head against the mighty oak, his punishment for being so gullible. The impression of bark on his forehead began to sting.

Adjusting his backpack, he was confident that Reagan had coordinated this reception from Boston. *Hell, he probably took out ads in the local newspaper. "High Hope Reforms Wayward Child Star." That'll drive attendance.* And it almost worked too, but not this night. They weren't that smart, he told himself, feeling the sudden weight of his backpack as he adjusted the straps.

The strange thing was that Clay was usually able to tell a person's intentions by looking into their eyes. He prided himself on it. Sitting in that jail, he hadn't seen it. Reagan had pulled off the impossible: insincere sincerity.

Turning away from the church, he decided to make a run for it. Retracing the winding mountain road in his head, he just hoped he would be able to find his way in the dark. Just as he was about to dart down the hill, he heard the haunting music of bagpipes coming from the church.

Bagpipes…? He half expected a brass band, trumpets …something assembled for a supermarket opening, but bagpipes?

His eyes welled up with a mixture of anger and fear as the music seeped in. It was a fitting score to the events of the last week, capable of stirring his anger before settling into the disappointment that always remained.

He had actually believed that someone cared about him. As his green eyes widened, the sudden glow of headlights crossed his path. Turning his head, Clay was awestruck by what he discovered.

A black hearse moved slowly across the expansive lawn. News cameras were positioned on either side, filming as it moved to the church.

Clay watched in confusion. He felt guilty that he hadn't anticipated this scene, that he had assumed that the media had turned out to see him. Clay wasn't self-absorbed. It was just that he learned early on that the world revolved around him, so it was more a revelation than anything else. Seeing all the reporters and news vans, it was understandable that he would think that tonight's spotlight was for him. *Who else could garner such a turnout?* A chill raced through his body as he realized the possibility of who lay in that casket. *Not Reagan?* Clay had known there was something not right about Reagan in that jail cell, but this?

The hearse parked at the far side of the church. He watched as the pallbearers unloaded the casket. Once it was inside, the glaring lights from all the media went out.

The church was now illuminated by its own light, a few discreet fixtures that cast the structure in a warming glow. It looked modest now, but more inviting, standing out from the darkness that surrounded it.

The media had gotten their money shot and were packing up for the night. Clay knew it was just a matter of time before they headed his way. He thought about jetting down the hill while he could, but he needed to know if Reagan was really in that casket.

Pulling his knit hat lower and avoiding direct eye contact, he navigated himself around the news vans and camera crews. Soon he was on his hands and knees, having ducked into the nearby shrubbery. Tyler wasn't the only one who had skills maneuvering unnoticed. Clay was the original phantom kid. Burt would be screaming for Clay as the whole set waited, unaware that he was crawling along the rafters above or curled up in a hanging black curtain behind the set. Clay took pride in knowing that he could be right next to the guy and he wouldn't even know it. There would always be a steep price to pay for disappearing, but Clay felt that those few moments of being invisible were well worth it. Clay now emerged from a row of bushes and discretely slipped into the church through a side door.

Catching his breath, he cautiously stepped into the lobby and was relieved to find it empty. Everyone was inside now.

The towering sanctuary doors rumbled from the composition playing within. They were hand carved from oak and together formed a twisted, wind-bent tree. The robust trunk stretched into a series of narrow branches with leaves blowing in the wind. He could only imagine what was behind those doors.

He moved toward them, almost flush with the grain. Running his fingers along the grooves, he thought about the irony of killing a tree to carve a picture of one.

Grasping the iron handle, he told himself that he would just take a peek and be out of there as fast as he had arrived. Increasingly curious, Clay carefully cracked open the door.

The sea of blackness filled the sanctuary, standing rows of dark suits and dresses spilling into the aisles. Side by side they stood, their backs blocking his view, forcing his anxious eyes to rise above the congregation.

Television monitors lined the walls, obscuring the ornate stained glass windows. A larger screen, a Jumbotron, was positioned on the far side of the altar, offsetting the wooden cross. Clay gripped the door handle tighter.

Now, as the crowd was seated, Clay could see in person what he had watched on screen. White roses draped the simple cedar casket as it moved down the aisle. It was perched on the vast altar, surrounded by rose bushes in stone urns. Bagpipers lined one side of the aisle, while an orchestra was assembled on the other.

Holding the door steady, Clay felt its weight increasingly apparent as he gazed at the coffin. *Tell me he's not inside that thing.* He thought about stepping inside to find out, but he just stood at the door, unwilling to cross that threshold.

Whatever reality was in there he didn't want to enter it. So Clay did what he had grown accustomed to doing. Letting go of the rustic iron handle, he stepped back, allowing the sturdy door to close silently, and his eyes once more left staring at the elaborate tree carving.

He stood there, as if shutting the door had separated

him from the reality he didn't want to discover. He wanted to leave right then, but he needed to know who was in that coffin. Stepping away from the door, he noticed a sign that read: "Balcony Closed." Recalling Tyler's sage advice, Clay stepped over the velvet rope.

Chapter Twelve

Ascending the narrow staircase, Clay stepped on the partially carpeted wooden steps and emerged in the balcony loft. It was empty apart from a small tech crew running the light and sound board that glowed in the dark. Luckily, the college-age technicians were too distracted to bother with him.

Clay noticed a tattered curtain gently blowing as it covered the stained glass window to keep out the light. The cold night breeze from the open window brushed against his face as he hesitated in the back of the loft, trying not to imagine the man he hoped would rescue him lying in that coffin.

He moved forward, below an ominous crack that brazed the ceiling and skirted the central beam. Stepping over twisted cables and extension cords that crossed his path, he realized that the site could pass for a long ignored crime scene. Moving toward the railing, the thoughts churned in his mind.

Clay felt horrible for thinking Reagan had set him up, especially after everything he had done for him.

He had promised himself that he wouldn't get his hopes up, but he did. He did get his hopes up. Somewhere between the jail cell and the plane ride, he started to believe that what Reagan described was real. Now he feared all that hope was sealed in that cedar casket. Leaning over the railing, he stared down at the service below, searching for Reagan, terrified at what he might discover.

* * *

In the green room, Ted Mitchell stared into the oval mirror, struggling with his tie. His eyes were once more distracted by his father's ever-present reflection in the glass.

Reagan stood several feet away holding Ted's suit jacket.

"You're timing is so convenient," Ted said, frustrated as he undid the uneven knot. They were the first words he had spoken to his father since his return. "I should have known."

"Son…"

"Don't talk to me. I don't want to hear it."

Ted had practiced the eulogy, hastily piecing it together from memorable tributes he had heard over the years. Growing up in a church, you attend a lot of funerals. It was the sort of tribute he had waited his whole life to give, but it would not be read. It would remain folded in his suit pocket. His father would now be doing the honor. Being replaced last minute always upset Ted, but this was unforgivable.

Reagan looked at his watch, put down Ted's jacket and walked over behind him. Without asking, he calmly reached around and began to re-tie Ted's tie. Reagan's face was clearly reflected in the mirror. "The secret is line up both sides…over, then under…"

Normally, when Ted wore a tie it was under a robe so he didn't have to worry about the length being even.

"Quinn always did this for me," Ted admitted, patting down his groomed head of sandy-blonde hair.

"Everything changes after tonight," Reagan said softly, staring into the mirror. "Everything has already changed."

"I would have been fine without you. You do know that?" Ted wanted his father to agree.

"We all need a little help," Reagan said, tightening the tie just below Ted's neck. Their grieving eyes glanced up now, staring at themselves in the oval mirror, a telling portrait of father and son.

Reagan's assistant entered, wearing a headset and holding a clipboard. "The church is packed."

Reagan turned to Ted, "Are you ready?"

Ted took a deep breath.

* * *

Watching from the balcony railing, Clay waited

anxiously. Finally, the door on the far side of the altar opened. The crowd rose to their feet. Clay jerked forward to see who would enter.

Reagan emerged from the door, his stoic face filling the television monitors. The camera stayed on him as he walked the length of the altar, the lens ignoring Ted, who followed a few paces behind.

Clay sunk into his seat, relieved to see Reagan. In fact, it wasn't until he exhaled that he realized how upset he had become. He felt like an idiot getting so worked up. Sliding deeper into the crushed velvet seat, his eyes glanced at the nearest monitor. All Reagan had done was walk across the altar, and he had already captivated the crowd. *This guy is indestructible.*

Ted took the pulpit.

Looking into the monitor, Clay stared at Ted's close-up. It had been years, but he looked exactly the same, only taller and more polished… like a wax figure from Madame Tussaud's. You could stare into his eyes all day and still not know what was behind them. "Bad lighting," Clay mumbled under his breath. Although the pulpit lights were probably positioned for Reagan, Clay thought Ted would appear unnatural in any set-up. He looked like he was doing a poor imitation of his father.

Reaching into his bag for the M&M's he bought at the airport, Clay tore the package open and popped one in his mouth. Whoever was in that casket must be important.

Looking up, he took another look at the huge crack in

the plaster. Several inches wide, it ran across the balcony, supporting the roof. *Earthquake damage?* He realized that the gaping crack was only visible from the balcony or perhaps by those standing in the pulpit, but went unseen by the scores of people who faced the altar below. He wondered if the people below were in danger…if another shake could finish the job?

Clay was confident that whatever money was not spent fixing structural damage was spent out front on technology. "I thought there was no television in Cliff Falls?" he mumbled under his breath, recalling Reagan's assuring sales pitch. The church was filled with televisions.

Ted was halfway through the 23rd Psalm when Clay realized he hadn't heard a word Ted said. Clay felt sorry for the grieving family. Certainly, Ted wasn't doing the job.

Clay evaluated the production value of the event, forgetting that this was real, that someone had actually died. It was like when Clay would watch a monitor on set. Although he would be in full makeup and costume, he would become so engrossed that, for a moment, he would forget that it was happening live, just a few feet away, and think he was in his living room. Clay wouldn't realize he was actually on set until someone messed up or until he'd hear the director yell "cut." Then he would snap out of it.

"This isn't so scary."

Clay turned abruptly; the child's voice was in earshot.

Tyler stood in the aisle, his dress shirt wrinkled, his hair ruffled, his pants dirt stained. He now looked like a boy his age should, except for the hesitation in his eyes.

"Is the box open?"

Recognizing the boy's fear, he looked over the balcony and then back at the boy. "It's closed...I promise."

"Everyone is here because of my grandmother."

"I'm...sorry." Clay didn't know what else to say. And somehow sorry didn't seem to be enough. At a loss for words, Clay offered Tyler some M&M's, but the boy didn't want any. It wasn't that Clay wasn't sorry; it was just that there are different kinds of sorry. Clay was sorry in the way a person is when they hear about trapped miners on the evening news. Sorry from the comfort and safety of your living room as opposed to the sorry you feel standing outside the mine. Clay tried to stay clear of the mine.

The boy bravely looked out over the balcony, exhaling at what he didn't see. Sinking into his seat, he plopped his arm onto Clay's armrest.

Bothered, Clay stared at the boy's arm on his armrest. "Aren't you supposed to be with your mother?"

"She's in New Jersey...Graduate school," the boy said remorsefully. Cocking his head, he pointed over the balcony. "I'm supposed to be down there."

Glancing in that direction, Clay assumed that "down there" meant in the first few rows of the church, but Tyler was pointing to the empty chair on the altar beside his father and grandfather.

Kicking off his penny loafers, Tyler stretched out his toes. He had been running all night because he didn't want to be up front. Not on this night, not when he was sad. He knew that he'd be in trouble the next day, but he didn't care. Besides he was usually in trouble.

Reagan took the pulpit. Everyone in the crowd seemed to sit up straighter, including Clay and Tyler.

Although he was solemn, Reagan's face radiated in the monitors. He didn't need good lighting, he came with his own. His mere presence inspired confidence. "Forty years ago we came to Cliff Falls with little more than a dream. Today each of you is part not only of that dream, but our family."

"That's my grandfather," Tyler said proudly, pointing with his penny loafer.

Clay pulled his eyes away from the screen. "That's your grandfather?"

"Yup," Tyler said smirking.

Clay felt a lead ball in his stomach, realizing that he was attending Rose Mitchell's funeral. His recollection of her was good…kind…very kind. She was the grounded counterpart to Reagan's inspirational ways.

She had found him one night crying after a scuffle with Burt on the tour. No one else knew what was going on or, if they did, they never let on, but she knew. He was embarrassed that she found him like that, but in that moment he knew he could trust her. He was angry when she called his mom, but knew she did it because she cared about him. When his mom called that night he thought she finally developed a spine, but then Burt twisted everything around, some explanation about Clay needing discipline and a strong male role model. She backed down. Ted was lucky to have a real mom.

He felt guilty having thought Reagan had manipulated him, that he was only interested in exploiting his fame. When in reality, the man had arrived back from Boston only to discover his wife had died. It did occur to Clay that people who manipulate and exploit others also lose spouses, but at this point he was giving Reagan the benefit of the doubt. Clay stared at Reagan's glossy steel eyes in the monitor, now recognizing that same frailty he had seen in that jail cell in Boston.

"Now we are sad…" Reagan seemed lost for a moment, staring at the flower draped coffin, "…but our hope remains high." Reagan lifted his head in a sweeping movement, raising his chin above the crowd, proudly echoing the sentiment. "Our hope remains high!"

"Fade to black…" Clay overheard the tech crew whisper behind him.

As the house lights faded, Clay squeezed his wrinkled bag of M&M's, his eyes straining, adjusting to the darkness. Bagpipes played as flickering home movies appeared on screen.

Clay and Tyler sat side-by-side, like two kids in the movie balcony, captivated by the tribute footage celebrating the life of Rose and the history of High Hope. The black-and-white childhood images, dancing with specs, blossomed into the muted colors of faded home movies; groundbreaking, construction, the birth of Ted. They merged into the harshly lit video clips of the eighties and nineties; prayer meetings, book signings, family gatherings, the birth of Tyler. The anthem built, the sweeping music intensifying, but refusing to crest.

Instead of watching the television monitors, Clay found himself focused on the only remaining darkness in the sanctuary; the only patch out of reach from the glare of the televisions. Through the dim light of the church, Clay watched a stoic Reagan and Ted mourn.

Clay resisted what was welling up inside of him, trying not to get overwhelmed or to feel too deeply. But it was no use. Reality set in. He felt himself crossing the threshold, connecting with the life, pain and grief of this church. He wasn't simply watching it; he was entering it, somehow standing outside the mine, waiting for word that they would be alright.

"That's my mom!" Tyler pointed at the Jumbotron in the distance.

Clay's eyes rose to the massive screen above Reagan and Ted. The digital image was so clear that it was lifelike. The vivid footage was of a family picnic. Rose was laughing in the brightness of the afternoon sun. Tyler and his mother fought over a slice of watermelon. Tugging back and forth, his mother resorted to tickling the boy. The boy was laughing, but refusing to let go.

"That's my mom," Tyler quietly repeated, mesmerized by his mother's image in the distance.

Pulling his eyes away from the screen, Clay watched the boy beside him, recognizing something familiar, too familiar in his eyes....

His tears were obscured by the steady beads of rain traveling down the bus station window, his mother's image fading in the distance. She moved towards the bus, ticket gripped in hand, her words repeating in his head.

"It's not forever. I'm in the way."

A moment ago, she was beside him. Now she was leaving. As she turned to walk away, he had tried to follow, but had felt a callous hand on his shoulder holding him back; "No!" the boy screamed, his objection fogging up the glass. "No!"

But there was nothing he could do. Through that blurry, rain-soaked window, Clay watched his mother get on the bus, her last words haunting him for years to come.

"They are going to take good care of you. I promise."

Suddenly, the doors shut and the bus drove away.

"That was my mom," Tyler said softly, the image fading from the screen.

"I know."

This moment became real, too real, for Clay, no longer an observer, overwhelmed by Tyler longing for his mother. He wasn't standing outside the mine, he was in it, trapped, gasping for air. He never wanted to enter that place again. His heart was pounding, his survival instincts telling him to leave. Reaching for his duffel bag, he rose to his feet.

Since the night of the fire, he had arranged his whole life to never feel this kind of pain again, and he was not going to start now. He didn't sign up for this.

"You're leaving?" Tyler didn't have to wait for the answer. He knew.

"I've stayed too long already."

Turning to leave, his eyes returned to the ominous

jagged crack that skirted the central beam and loomed over the balcony. He had been so distracted watching the monitors that he had forgotten all about it.

Clay reluctantly reached into his back pocket, retrieving Tyler's neck tie, placing it on the armrest beside the boy.

"I'm sorry."

Tyler looked at the tie.

Struggling to maintain his composure, Clay waved goodbye to Tyler, and then left, descending the staircase and stepping into the lobby.

Determined not to return, Clay slipped out of the church. As music poured out of the sanctuary, Clay Grant walked into the night.

Chapter Thirteen

"She was the life of this church."

Ted embraced the next mourner, his eyes aware of the ever-growing crowd that waited in line to offer condolences. It was endless. He wanted to be anywhere but here. He wondered who was being comforted.

With each hug, he felt the folded eulogy on the inside of his suit pocket press up against his chest. It had not even been read and somehow it was repeatedly being stuffed back into his heart. It was a steady and familiar reminder from the crowd. One that undermined every 'sorry' that he heard. From now on, he would keep everything that close.

Ted held each embrace as long as he could; it minimized the conversation and allowed the backed-up line to move along. Besides, the sentiments and questions were becoming predictable.

"Where's Quinn?"

"She missed her flight," Ted assured the inquirer, nodding his head with disappointment. He could tell that other people in line were listening in. "She had gone back for the first day of classes."

"Quinn is lucky to have such a supportive husband."

Ted held the smile as long as he could. It was another awkward moment extended by the backed-up line. *That* he blamed on his father.

Reagan stood a few feet away, unaware that he was the cause of the slow moving line and Ted's awkward moments. He was working the crowd as only Reagan could, and as usual they loved it. He was careful to not just hug the mourners, but to touch each one on the shoulder, look into their eyes, and receive what they had to say. He gave each mourner the sort of personal attention that allowed them to walk away feeling filled up. He had a reputation as "Comforter in Chief."

But Ted knew his father. He could tell if Reagan was distracted even when others thought they had the pastor's his full attention. Reagan had a way of making people feel like he was in the middle of the storm with them, even though he was never anywhere near it. As the mourner finally moved down the line, Ted noticed a familiar gleam in his father's eyes. Ted was puzzled. Reagan was looking for someone in the crowd.

Ted was standing now, but the night everything happened, he had been running. *Tyler tried to keep up as Ted urgently raced down the hospital corridor, his father's voice-mail trailing in his head. "It's time."*

Pressing the elevator button again, he didn't want to miss the last moments. As they approached the nurse's station, Tyler spotted a physician, but Ted already knew. The thick door was cracked open, the foot of the bed peeking out from the hanging curtain. It was too late. After all the days and hours Ted had spent at the hospital, in the end he was too late.

Staring at the door, he hesitated before moving forward. He could hear Tyler behind him, crying, comforted by the nurse.

Ted cautiously opened the door and crossed the threshold, the stale hospital smell overwhelming him. He drew back the curtain. Her body was covered with a white sheet. Approaching the bed, his disposition was that of a scared child trying to be brave. Reaching out, he tugged at the linen covering her face. What he saw was his own face reflected back at him, the narrow nose and rounded cheek bones. Ted stared at his mother's lifeless body; the woman who gave him life, suddenly gone.

Full of confusion, Ted looked up and turned to the nurse who was entering the room. He had one question. "Where's my father?"

Chapter Fourteen

The bell jingled as Clay opened the glass door and stepped into the Acorn Diner, the chill of the night lingering on his face. His troubled eyes tried to hold back everything he was feeling inside. He had seen the diner's light from the top of the hill as he made his way down Ridge Road on foot. Only a few cars had passed him, so he was certain that he was ahead of the crowd.

Most establishments in Cliff Falls were closed for the night. The modest downtown was dark, except for the warming glow emanating from the Acorn Diner. It was always open late. Located at the prominent intersection of Cliff Falls Drive and Ridge Road, the yellow ranch-style building was hard to miss.

A counter ran the length of the establishment, flanked by plate-glass windows that framed the activity off each street: the one that ran through the city and the other that led up to the church. Folks eating the same food inside the same diner could have entirely different experiences depending upon which window they were looking out. Cliff Falls Drive was usually busy, bustling with people and cars, while Ridge Road was slower and rustic, lined with towering oaks. You could enter the diner from either side, although most people exited the door they entered.

At this hour, the streets looked the same. There was only darkness outside as mourners began trickling in. The Acorn had gotten word about the rescheduled funeral service and its unusual time, so they were expecting a crowd once the service let out. Clay gripped his duffel bag as the door slowly shut. All he needed now was a phonebook and a place to wait until the cab arrived.

There was an empty seat at the counter, but Clay wasn't in the mood for small talk. He spotted a booth on the opposite side of the diner beneath the window that faced Cliff Falls Drive. He'd wait for his cab there. He knew people would be coming in the Ridge Road side of the diner and wanted to be as far away from it as possible. Reaching for a menu, he made his way across the room.

An art-deco mural adorned the wall above the counter. It depicted the town's early days: the intersection of Cliff Falls Drive and Ridge Road in the 1930's. Even back then the streets were different. Clay assumed the building had been a feed store. Technically it still was, just a different kind of feed and flock.

The mural's red and golden tones resembled the bountiful labels you'd find on the side of fruit crates from that era, but with almost a political message of brotherhood. It featured the rustic faces of city workers and ranch hands crossing paths in front of the feed store, the painted sun rays shining down on both. Clay had seen similar style murals on the east coast, but nothing with this landscape. He admired it, but wondered if the diversity was representative of the time or imposed by the idealism of the artist.

Tossing his duffel bag on one side of the booth, he loosened the straps on his backpack, the shifting of its weight causing his tired eyes to look upward. It was a glimpse of Heaven. Maybe the only Heaven he would ever know. The ceiling was littered with a multitude of colorful toothpicks apparently placed there with the assistance of a straw and some hot air. Their gleaming cellophane glare was a welcome comfort to the ever increasing sea of blackness as mourners began pouring in. Apparently, Clay wasn't as far ahead of the crowd as he thought.

Quickly settling into the booth, he slid all the way in until he was up against the window. Propping his menu up on one side of him, he reached for the Venetian blind and lowered it. Gazing out the window as the blinds inched down, his breath on the glass was proof that his heart was still racing. He had come all this way. He felt terrible skipping out on Reagan, but he couldn't help it, and besides, what did the guy expect? Clay stared into the darkness. He couldn't see it, but he knew the city was out there. Not just the town, but the city below. Right now that was easier to believe in than anything that might lay further up the mountain. As Clay pulled the other cord, the wooden blinds shut. His makeshift fortress was complete.

Lowering his head, his weary eyes were drawn to the shiny silverware on a paper placemat that read 'Acorn Diner.' The knife and spoon reflected the colorful toothpicks overhead, specs of blue, green, yellow and red light dancing in the silver-plated utensils. The cheap silverware looked beautiful.

He wondered if he were to move it, at what point it would lose its reflection. Not one to leave well enough alone, he carefully picked up the knife, tilting it from side to side. But the colorful light glistened all the more. For each spec that would seemingly fall off the utensil's edge, another would appear to take its place.

Clay was mesmerized by the light, but rather than looking up, he stared deeper into the knife, tilting it forward, moving further into his fortress. Suddenly, the colorful lights vanished before his eyes, replaced by an elongated face trapped beneath water spots not previously noticed. Once again, he had gotten in the way. Gripping the knife tighter, he stared at his distorted image. Whatever Heaven was trying to tell him, he wasn't getting the message.

As he lowered the knife, another face miraculously appeared in the blade.

"Coffee…?"

Focusing on the silverware, he was careful not to make eye contact. "Please. I'm in a rush."

The waitress turned over the porcelain cup. "Do you know what you want?"

He raised his head above the propped up menu. It was another glimpse of Heaven.

All Clay saw were eyes. At first he didn't even realize they were hazel, just that they were bright, radiating warmth that overshadowed anything else in the room. Clay watched as the brightness was interrupted as she lowered her gaze to pour the coffee. He found himself waiting for her to look up again. As she did, he lowered the menu. Maybe he did have time for a quick bite?

She smiled again, waiting for his response.

"Got any pastry?" Clay noticed her name tag as he stumbled over his words.

Becky pointed to the pastry case. It was loaded with cakes and pies. "What are you in the mood for?"

"What do you recommend?" He smiled, trying to muster up some charm.

"Tiramisu…It's our specialty."

"Italian or some California version…?" Clay was suspicious. California had destroyed pizza with ham and pineapple. He didn't want to consider what it had done to tiramisu.

"Well our pastry chef is Italian, but he's also from California, so I don't know what to tell you."

"I'll take my chances." Clay was tempted to order more than dessert, but he had already stayed here too long.

Reaching into his pocket, he searched for some change. "Do you have a phonebook? I need to call a cab."

"It's behind the counter. Help yourself."

Sliding out of the booth, Clay apprehensively made his way to the counter. Aside from the waitresses, he was the only one not wearing black, which made him stand out all the more. Reaching under the counter, he retrieved the phonebook, quickly returning to the privacy of his booth.

Becky brought the tiramisu and set it in front of Clay before hurrying to respond to another customer.

He looked at it puzzled. Obviously, this was not Mike's Pastry. Clay took a bite, frowned, and then pushed it aside. It was time to cut his losses and get out of this place. He reached for the phonebook. The Cliff Falls Yellow Pages had a glossy picture of the rushing falls on the cover. "PhotoShop," he mumbled under his breath. He was doubtful that there were any falls in the town at all. It was probably just a clever marketing ploy some city manager came up with long ago to attract tourists.

Another wave of mourners arrived, settling into the booth behind Clay.

Flipping through the pages, he overheard their conversation.

"Does Ted remind you of Al Gore?"

Someone else laughed.

"When the old man goes, I don't know how that place can survive."

Clay hated gossip having been the object of it his whole

life. He prided himself on never listening to it, whether it was about himself or someone else. Turning the page, he spotted an advertisement for a taxi company.

"You know my daughter works at the hospital. Apparently, after Rose died Reagan just up and disappeared. Ted was livid. He couldn't find Reagan anywhere."

Clay clenched the phonebook, but leaned back in spite of himself. He couldn't help but listen.

"That's why the funeral was tonight. They waited as long as they could. They almost had to hold it without Reagan."

Clay's jaw dropped, his body inching down the booth.

"I heard the same thing from some of the elders."

As Clay slid down the booth, his eyes rose until they were staring at the gleaming toothpicks overhead.

"Wherever he went it must have been important."

* * *

Reagan buttoned his pajamas, staring at the untouched bed. She insisted on making it before leaving for the hospital. That was how Rose was. She even laid out his clothes for the next day. The matching shirt and tie were still resting on the perfectly folded quilt that was draped over the bed's edge. For forty-three years he had slept beside her. *Forty-three years.* He told himself that once the funeral was over, then he'd be ready to sleep in it again. "The things we tell ourselves…" Reaching for his bathrobe, he made his way into his study.

Downstairs, the kitchen was filled with casseroles. No doubt they started arriving the night he left, along with a steady stream of comforting widows eager to be first in line. Reagan knew the drill. He had witnessed this ritual countless times, always vowing that he would never be on the receiving end. Luckily, he wasn't, at least not initially. For all the problems his disappearance caused, that was one benefit he was grateful for.

He had cleaned out his personal rainy day fund to pay for the third of Clay's debt that the court required. Now that it was raining in Reagan's own life, the money was useless anyhow.

Settling into his recliner in his study, he utilized his bathrobe as a blanket. He stared at a picture of Rose on the nearby desk. It was the same one used on the cover of the funeral program. He was glad Ted had chosen it. It was Reagan's favorite, although he could not remember where it was taken. But the place did not matter, nor the lavender dress that she was wearing. It was her eyes. Everything you needed to know about Rose, you could find there. And they were never clearer, except that last night.

Her eyes transcended everything, the sterile hospital room, the sickness, her failing body. Reagan could not imagine that that light would ever go out. Reagan had gently wiped her forehead with a moist cloth as the nurse administered the medication intravenously, the drops of fluid working their way into her system to offset the waves of pain and nausea. Skirting her brow with the cloth, he watched as she stared into the distance.

Before he could look away, Rose caught him. She looked right at him, attuned to his introspection and bothered by the special attention. "I'm not afraid. When God wants me, He wants me."

"Well, right now we want you." Reagan wasn't one to concede a challenge, even one that had long been decided. He resumed wiping her brow, discreetly glancing at the nurse.

"She should be feeling this soon," the nurse assured him.

Rose rolled her tired eyes. She couldn't understand it. Death was a part of life. To her it was a natural progression, one that she had made peace with long ago.

"Death isn't scary... living is," Rose said, scolding Reagan and the nurse, "Nobody can escape it."

"Death and taxes..." Reagan said, conferring with the nurse.

"Life... nobody escapes life," Rose corrected them.

Reagan knew Rose was right. She usually was. Her weakness only made that strength more apparent.

Rose reached out and touched his hand. "You're holding him back. He'll never be a man until you let him fail and learn to pick himself up."

Reagan would do anything for her, but this was one request that put everything they had built in jeopardy.

Resting her eyes, the medication began to take effect. "Nobody escapes life."

He watched as she began to drift. Reagan wanted to escape everything that he knew was coming. If he was honest,

*that's what he wanted to do, but he wasn't going to leave
Rose. She was his girl and the one who always held him
together. Now who would comfort the comforter?*

*Reagan knew how to be a visionary and he knew how
to help people, but this he didn't know how to deal with.
The idea that she was slipping from his grasp made him
feel powerless, and he hated that. And it made him want
to run.*

"That's you…" The nurse pointed to the television,
reaching for the volume control, "…you and your son!"

*Reagan looked up, recognizing himself on the TV. He
had not seen the footage in years.*

"Here is one of his last public appearances at the
Orange Bowl in Miami."

Reagan, Clay and Ted stood on the stage together.

"Boys what do you do when someone asks you to
take drugs?"

"Just say no!" *Clay and Ted shouted.*

"I'll go find your son," *the nurse said as she left the room.*

*Rose opened her eyes and focused on what was a blurry
photograph of a man completely covered in flour.*

"Fifteen years after the mysterious fire, have we
finally found 'Little Guy Mike'? We have an insider in
Boston investigating the assault charges to confirm
whether this is real or just another Clay Grant rumor."

*Rose looked at Reagan, shaking her head. He knew
that look.*

"Maybe it's not him?" *Reagan reasoned, sensing Rose's
concern. He didn't want her to get upset.*

"I know those eyes." She pointed to the screen, fighting off the effects of the medication. "It's not human how they continue to exploit that child. We should have done something. Some adult should have done something."

"I've often thought that, but I still don't know what I could have done." Reagan watched as Rose struggled to stay awake.

"If I was able, I would fly there and help the boy myself."

"I believe you would," Reagan said as the memory faded. "I believe you would."

Pulling the bathrobe tighter under his neck, Reagan wondered if he could make good on either promise. He fell asleep in the recliner gazing at the silver-framed picture of Rose.

* * *

Breathless, Clay returned to the church on foot and found the parking lot empty. All the cars were gone now. The only evidence of what had occurred were a few discarded programs with Rose's portrait on the cover scattered on the gravel pavement, her knowing eyes welcoming him back.

His first instinct was to gather the programs and place them somewhere, anywhere else, but somehow he felt it was a greater sign of respect to leave them there undisturbed. Some things, he reasoned, should not be so easily forgotten.

Crouching down, he picked one up for himself, noting the date. August 16th. She died on his birthday.

Turning his attention back up the hill, he made his way along the steep path, the sound of his breath breaking the night's silence. Approaching the crest, he hesitated, somehow surprised by the darkness that met him. The church's own fixtures were on a timer and were off for the night. It was almost as if the church were sleeping, resting for what would come in the morning.

Grasping the handle to the outside sanctuary doors, he rattled it, but found it locked. This time he was literally left out in the cold. Even if he wasn't too tired to walk back to town, he knew that it was too late to find lodging for the night. He had to find another way. That's when his survival instincts kicked in.

Making his way around the perimeter of the church, he spotted a storage shed. Perhaps he'd find a tarp or something he could use as a blanket? He tried to open it, and to his amazement, not only was it unlocked, but a folded blanket with a new package of beef jerky sat waiting on the shelf. He smiled, grateful for the fool who forgot to lock it.

Settling on a bench next to the church steps, he gnawed on the beef jerky, unzipping his duffel bag. Putting on an extra sweatshirt and sweats over his jeans, he was still cold, so he put on another two shirts. Pulling his knit hat below his ears, he bundled up in the blanket. Leaning back, he rested his head on his duffel bag, which doubled as a pillow.

The sky was clear, each star fixed into position like an obvious map he could never decipher. He gazed upon the sky's majesty realizing how only an hour before he would have settled for cellophane toothpicks lodged in a ceiling.

For a moment he felt like he was right where he was supposed to be. Despite everything that had or would happen, this night he was supposed to be here, on this bench, under this sky. That much he knew. With his head nestled on his duffel bag, Clay Grant fell asleep under the watchful stars.

* * *

Deep in an alley in the North End, there was a quiet rumbling emanating from inside a dumpster. Burt Cummings sorted through the discarded scraps of shredded documents from the Boston Courthouse, searching for a lead before someone else found one. There was no way he was giving up now. He was enraged at himself for letting Clay slip through his fingers. Now everyone was looking for his cash cow, and he wasn't about to let the rest of the media cash in on Clay after he did all the leg work. It was Burt who kept the pressure on him all those years, ensuring that they got the best performance out of him. He told himself to be patient. He knew how Clay operated. There was no way he disappeared without leaving a trail. Under the cover of darkness, Burt dug through the mound of scraps, determined to find what he was looking for.

Chapter Fifteen

With heavy eyelids, Clay resisted the first signs of morning. The sun braised the side of his face, cutting the chill that enveloped the rest of his body. It had been a cold night, and he wasn't yet thawed. A cool breeze swept over him. He was unsure where he was, like a traveling salesman who forgot what city he was in. He felt wooden planks under his back. *Tell me I'm not drifting at sea?* All the more reason to sleep in, he thought clenching his eyes. As the rays intensified, he rolled over on the bench, his ears attuned to the rapid hissing of sprinklers in the distance. It was a gentle alarm clock allowing him to awake at his own pace.

Stepping out of his flatbed truck, Diego Marquez spotted a man asleep on the bench. Always the first on property, he was used to discovering stranded travelers.

Not too many homeless — the church was too removed for that. Hikers who misjudged the distance between the Peninsula and Half Moon Bay would occasionally set up camp for the night. They seemed to stumble upon the church just when they were too exhausted or lost to continue. The church was well positioned for just this event, but for liability reasons, he was supposed to move them along.

As Diego shut the door, he saw the familiar blanket tossed on the ground. He was glad this traveler found it. He knew the nights could get pretty cold, so he always kept one in the storage shed on the south side of the church for them to find. The staff was not always comfortable with their "overnight guests," but Diego had a soft spot for wanderers. At thirty-seven, he felt a church caretaker should do more than just set up chairs and maintain the grounds. Reaching into his truck, he retrieved a plaid thermos and approached the bench.

"Welcome to hotel High Hope," Diego said, careful not to startle the man.

Clay reluctantly opened one eye as an Aztec face came into focus. The guy looked angelic with the sun at his back, his muscular build only undermined by the sparkle in his eye. Clay squinted as the sun emerged through the golden oak leaves overhead. It was all coming back to him now.

"I hate to tell you this, but you're in the line of fire." Diego pointed to the opposite end of the bench.

Clay raised his head only to discover his jeans were

soaked from an over-reaching sprinkler. Plopping his head back into the duffel bag, he clenched his eyes as the rain-bird drenched his lower half.

"Some coffee will warm you up," Diego assured him, holding out the thermos. Twisting off the top, which doubled as a cup, he opened the container. The burnt aroma smelled like the inside of a donut shop.

Clay half expected an apple fritter. Stretching out his arms, he let out a discomforting yawn as he attempted to straighten his spine. "Maybe you should pour it on my back?"

Diego laughed, filling the plastic cup. "It's not gourmet, but it will do the trick."

"Are you sure there's enough?"

"There's plenty." Smiling, Diego handed him the cup.

Clay lazily sat up, making an effort to remove himself from the sprinkler's reach. Sipping the coffee, he stared at his surroundings. It all looked too perfect. The mountainous scenery was beautiful. The vast landscape basked in the morning light, while the towering trees provided patches of protective shade along the rolling hillside. This was the first time he was seeing it in the daytime. Everything was greener and more rustic than he had imagined. He stared at this new world, wondering if it would last or if it would come to an end as abruptly as everything else he had known.

"Just passing through?"

"I don't know." It was as truthful an answer as he could give. Nursing the coffee, he heard the crunching of tires on gravel. The sound overshadowed the hissing sprinklers.

"That's the boss."

Clay saw an SUV pulling into the upper parking lot.

"Don't worry. I'll take care of this." Handing him the thermos, Diego approached the vehicle.

Reagan opened the car door, hesitating the way a man hesitates on the side of the bed in the morning. This would be his last hesitation for the day. He knew he couldn't afford another, not if he was going to hold the church together. In a few hours he would face everything he set in motion and was doubtful he would have much to show for it. But Reagan was resilient. He always found a way.

"Didn't think you were coming in today," Diego said. He was usually the one to ask the direct question everyone else skirted. It was just his way, and without agenda. Most of the staff would never say the obvious, partially out of respect, partially out of self-motive, but Diego figured honesty was the best form of respect.

"If I didn't get out of bed this morning, I might never," Reagan confided. Reaching for his briefcase, Reagan stepped out of the SUV, squinting as the emerging sun reflected off the car door. In the distance, he saw a disheveled man sitting on the bench.

"Don't worry about him," Diego said, "he was just—"

Reagan smiled as the sleepy-eyed rag-a-muffin came into focus. Hope had arrived.

Clay offered a tired wave, yawning.

Diego realized that they knew each other.

Reagan made his way across the lawn, his confident stride giving little indication of the grief he was carrying. Last night Clay needed to know if this guy was alive. Now all he wanted to know was why Reagan flew 3,000 miles to help him right after his wife had died and what any of this had to do with him. But as Reagan drew closer, all those questions became less important. He could see the grief hidden in his eyes. Clay took off his knit hat and patted down his hair, embarrassed by his own tousled appearance.

Reagan stood before him beaming. "I knew you'd come."

Rising from the bench, Clay struggled to find the appropriate words. Reaching into his back pocket, he retrieved the funeral program, holding it out in his hand. "I'm sorry."

Reagan glanced at the picture of Rose. "I know."

Clay didn't know what else to say, so he just waited, figuring Reagan would speak when he was ready. After a few moments he did.

"It was Rose…who insisted that the church be built facing the city. If we were not going to be in the city we must at least face it, she reasoned. She was very fond of you. Do you remember her?"

Clay nodded, recalling a gift she had given him. In those days people were always giving "Little Guy Mike" gifts, usually with a more expensive motive included in the card. But this one was different. "She gave me a leather notebook…a journal."

Reagan smiled, knowing it was a gesture typical of Rose.

"I remember looking at it disappointed, like 'what a crappy gift.' But that last summer, when everything went down, I found myself reaching for it more and more. I filled it cover to cover. I think I thought of her a little bit every time I wrote in it."

"She would be glad that you were here."

"Thank you for everything, for the money and for trusting me to show up. That meant a lot."

"Well, as I said, I'm planning on putting you to work."

"Doing what?"

"We'll get to that." Reagan noticed another car pulling into the upper parking lot. It was Ted. He knew he had to usher Clay away before Ted saw him.

Clay could tell Reagan was distracted. "So what happens now?"

"Everything…"

Clay looked at him puzzled.

"But first Diego is going to get you settled."

* * *

Diego unlocked the door to the studio loft. It was one of the few on campus and was tucked away in the back of the property above an old meeting room that pre-dated every structure except the old barn. It was a place of solitude, a writer's retreat where Reagan composed his earlier sermons and that first book that gained him national attention. But that was years ago. For the past two decades, it was residence to a steady stream of pastors and interns who were given housing in exchange for reduced compensation. Lately it sat empty.

"It's small but has all the basics."

As the door opened, Clay hoped for something more than that salt box in Boston with its porthole for a window. He wasn't disappointed.

Natural light filled the space, gleaming through the large window and off of the hardwood floors. Tossing his duffel bag and backpack on the twin bed, he briefly noted the night stand with an alarm clock that flashed "12:00 AM" and then a simple desk that sat beneath a vast window looking out over the hillside.

Moving to the window, the landscape was breathtaking, void of any man-made structures. At the base of the hillside, he could see a flowing creek, apparently originating from the elusive falls. Everything was starting to feel a little too good to be true.

"Good luck with that TV."

Clay turned. The light shined on the bulging glass. The old Zenith had seen better days. It was a relic from another era. Pliers rested on the wooden veneer, a necessity if you wanted to change the channel. It sat on a television stand with rabbit ears covered in aluminum foil

Diego took hold of the antenna. "Cliff Falls, the heart of the technology revolution, but we still can't get decent reception. We're supposed to wire it for cable, but it keeps getting cut from the budget."

"It's perfect," Clay said with holy reverence.

"The college pastor lived here. After the tech bust the church let a lot of staff go. The Peninsula still hasn't recovered. Are you a pastor?"

"Me?" Clay chuckled. He had been mistaken for many things in life, but a pastor was never one of them. "No. I'm not a pastor."

Before Diego could ask another question, Clay changed the subject. "So these falls…how do you get to them?"

"I could tell you, but you'd probably get lost."

"Huh?"

Diego tried to explain. "There used to be clear signs that a bunch of boy scouts carved years ago. They weren't fancy, but they were in the shape of an arrow and basically got you there and back."

"What happened to them?"

"Well they're still there, you just don't know it," Diego said, as he approached the window.

Clay was confused.

"As part of a beautification project, some committee decided to plant indigenous flowers around them to make them more appealing. When the shrubs matured, they grew over the signs. Now you could stare at them all day long and not know they were pointing somewhere. Don't get me wrong, the signs are beautiful. Tourists love to pose and take pictures in front of them. Unfortunately, they still get lost."

"So how do you find the falls?"

"The truth is you have to wander a bit. Wander and

listen for them."

Wandering was something Clay knew he was good at. Listening was another story. He looked down at his wet jeans from the sprinkler. "What time did Reagan say this staff meeting was again?"

"9:00." Diego checked his watch as he moved to the door. "If you hurry, you have time to take a hot shower."

Clay sat on the side of the bed and removed his shoes and wet socks as the shower heated up. He pressed his bare feet on the colorful oval rug. It had seen some wear, but its muted colors were vibrant enough to be welcoming and useful at the same time.

Undressing, he placed his dirty clothes in a pile on the floor. Stepping into the shower, he knew that he would have to be quick if he were going to make the meeting. The heat was stinging, penetrating the pressure in his back. Scrubbing, he tried his best to wash away the events of the past week. As the memories flooded back, Clay turned his face towards the powerful stream of water, forcing the thoughts from his mind.

Reaching for a towel, he placed it around his waist. Steam filled the bathroom, fogging up the medicine cabinet mirror above the vanity. Taking a face cloth, he wiped the mirror, catching a glimpse of his face before the steam returned, obscuring his reflection. He tried again, but each time, the steam returned.

Opening the bathroom door, he stepped into the living area. The steam poured out, traveling like breath across the room. Unzipping his duffel bag, he searched for some clean clothes. Most of what he brought with him, he had worn the night before to keep warm. As he removed a shirt, he noticed that the steam fogging up the vast window.

Moving toward the window, he was curious if he would still be able to see the stream at the base of the hillside. As he looked into the glass, he saw the stream flowing through his reflection.

* * *

The text went out, catching everyone off guard. The staff spilled out of their cubes and offices on the way to the conference room.

Alexis walked at a brisk pace down the corridor. Maggie, college intern and recent graduate of nearby Stanford University, trailed behind, busying herself with her Palm Pilot.

"Reagan's really here?" Max said with disbelief, emerging from his office dressed in obnoxious golfing attire. He was already on the course when he got the word.

"He's been in since seven."

"Ted too?"

"Ted too."

"Unbelievable…" Max pulled out his cell, leaving a voice mail. "Reagan came in after all. You'll have to play without me."

Thomas, worship director, stumbled out of his office wearing a brown sport coat as a dozen other staff members joined the group down the corridor. "Who comes to work the day after his wife's funeral?"

"His behavior hasn't exactly been predictable lately," Paul said.

"Lately...?" Monica said rolling her eyes.

Alexis shot Monica a look to keep her in line. "The man just lost his wife."

"You're the shrink Alexis. It's too early for him to come back to work. Didn't you advise him against it?" Max said.

"Deaf ears...Deaf ears..."

"Alexis said Reagan has an important announcement to make," Maggie said, looking up from her Palm Pilot.

"Maybe he's going to tell us where he went?"

* * *

Clay emerged from the loft with wet hair and a half-buttoned shirt. It was flannel and the only one he had left in his duffel bag. He was clean now, almost presentable. Unfortunately, he was also late.

Rushing down the steps, he ran through the rustic campus picking up speed, his feet pounding the dirt path. The air was invigorating.

Usually he was running from something. Only now did he consider what he was running to. He tried to imagine what he'd be doing, what he had to offer, or to what extent he'd have to interact with others. If he had his choice he'd be out in the fresh air working with Diego in the garden, getting his hands dirty. Once this formality of a staff meeting was out of the way, he'd feel better. *How bad could a staff meeting be?* He felt a pebble lodged in his shoe. Instead of stopping, he raced on, determined to ignore the repetitive sting in his heel.

Diego and a crew were busy planting rose bushes in the new garden Reagan had commissioned a few months ago. Set apart behind a whimsical gate, it had only been installed a few days earlier. It was a muddy mess. The flowerless bushes were all thorns and twisted stems covered in fresh dirt. Reaching for the hose, he spotted Clay coming down the hill.

"You're late," Diego shouted.

"I know. I know…" Clay shouted back.

"The church office is that way!" Diego pointed the hose in the other direction.

"Thank you!" Clay shouted, changing course.

Diego shook his head, amused by this latest addition to the church. Turning on the hose, he watered the shrubs, washing the dirt off the memorial headstone.

In the lower parking lot, Becky managed the tray of cranberry coffee cake as she shut the door to her Honda with her foot. It was still warm, steam trapped beneath the protective cellophane, with a note that read "High Hope/Staff Meeting – ASAP." One of these days she was going to get access to the upper lot. The Acorn had assumed the meeting was cancelled, so they were caught off-guard when the church called it in. Luckily, a tray was just coming out of the oven. Becky volunteered to run it up, just as she had volunteered to work the night before when everyone else was at the funeral. As the new hire, she preferred to volunteer rather than be told what to do, especially when she knew she'd end up doing a particular task anyway. Until she gained seniority, it was part of the job, and besides, volunteering made her popular with the other waitresses. She learned early on that those relationships were ultimately more important than fighting over something she could just as easily get done.

Becky made her way up the hill. The truth was she didn't mind deliveries, except when they took her away from the peak times when she made her best tips. The morning rush could be the difference between covering rent and affording those simple extras, like flowers and trips to the nail salon, that made her feel like a girl. She was surprised how important those little luxuries had become to her during the last year. Somehow they gave her the ability to deal with life's more mundane tasks, like carrying a tray of coffee cake up a sloping hillside. Nearing the crest, she forged ahead.

Picking up speed, she cut across the expansive lawn, determined to make it back before the end of the rush. The two-story building was just beyond the sanctuary. As she turned the corner, she looked up and saw a familiar face running straight towards her. As their eyes met, a collision seemed unavoidable. Becky gripped the tray of coffee cake in fear, her fingers clenching the metal rim....

Chapter Sixteen

Shifting his weight in a split-second reaction, Clay flew head over heels into the bushes, tossing and tumbling — branches absorbing the impact — and finally landing on his back as the dust kicked up.

"Are you alright?"

Standing over him were the same beautiful eyes from the night before. They stared at him with a look of concern.

"I'm fine...fine..." he coughed as the dust settled. "I think." Trying to save face, he rolled out of the bushes and onto his feet. Dusting off his pants, he picked leaves from his flannel shirt. He was no longer clean, now resembling a kid who had spent the day playing in the woods.

"Do you always run that fast?"

"I was on my way to staff meeting…"

"Wait, I know you. You're the tiramisu guy from last night."

Clay pulled twigs out of his hair, grateful she remembered him but unsure that he wanted to be associated with that tiramisu.

"I thought you were just passing through?"

"As it turns out, I've decided to stay…" he said regaining his composure. "…at least a little while longer."

"I'm Becky."

"Nice to meet you…Becky." He looked into her eyes slowly, deliberately, and held her gaze until she glanced away. Usually he wouldn't use his real name in a new place, but Reagan let it slip when he met Diego. "I'm Clay."

"Look, I'm usually not this forward," Becky said, "but I really have to get back to work and…"

"No, really, I appreciate women who take initiative." His confident tone bordered cockiness.

"You do?"

"I'm flattered." He put the palm of his hand on his chest in an attempt to seem modest.

"…about the coffee cake?"

"Huh…?"

"Coffee cake…" She looked down at the tray and then back at him. "You're going to staff meeting, right? I thought you could take it with you."

"Of course…coffee cake," he pointed to the tray trying to save face.

"If it's a problem…?"

"I'd be glad…flattered actually, to deliver it for you."

"Way to help a girl out." Becky smiled, handing him the tray.

As she walked away, Clay was left holding the coffee cake.

* * *

Spilling into the room, the staff took their seats. The conference room was on the second floor, just down the hall from Reagan and Ted's offices. A modest space, it boasted an oval table with plenty of seating and a bay window that looked out over the property. The sun reflected off the wood paneling. Although the reflection was distracting, the staff preferred to keep the curtains open so that they could gaze out over the landscape when staff meetings went long. This day, all eyes were on Reagan.

Glancing at the clock, Reagan addressed the staff. "She was the heartbeat of this church, and she thought so much of each of you."

Sipping coffee around the table, the staff listened intently. Reagan could see the loss of Rose visible in their eyes too. Hand picked for their ability and loyalty, the ministries they ran were mini-churches within the larger body, places where people got spiritually fed and felt a sense of community. Since the tech bust, the church had been enduring an ongoing financial crisis; everyone was feeling the pinch and everything was accomplished on the leanest of budgets. Although the church was forty-years-old, it felt like a startup without adequate funding, re-inventing itself at every turn in hopes of staying relevant. Now they just needed to know that Reagan could recover from this loss and continue to lead. Not just for their sake, but for the people they served. As he went on, Ted quietly slipped into the room, taking his seat beside his father.

"One thing we know about family is that they stick together, especially in challenging times."

As Ted sat down, he glanced at his father wondering if he understood the irony of what he was saying. They had all heard that his father disappeared the night his mother died and were curious where he went, but Ted didn't want to hear it. For Ted the where could never change the why....

Tuning his father out, Ted turned his thoughts to the sermon he was scheduled to give this Sunday. He only got to preach a few times a year, usually when his father was traveling or on obscure dates like the Sunday after Christmas or, in this case, the Sunday after his mother's funeral. Although he was barely speaking to his father, he assumed it was still a go, especially since he had to scrap the eulogy he had written. As a rule they never announced when Ted preached for fear it would affect attendance. Ted wished they would. He would rather preach to an empty church than deal with a packed house that had just been informed that an understudy would now be playing the lead role.

Reagan kept an eye on the door, waiting for Clay to show. "I am convinced that God has hidden gifts in our hearts, gifts we may not even know we have or see in each other. Rose always believed in you. We must be a family that believes in each other. That being said, I have an announcement to make. When Ted preaches this Sunday, he will be doing so as Senior Pastor."

Ted looked up in disbelief, questioning if he heard his father correctly.

"It's time to think about succession," Reagan said.

The staff was frozen in disbelief. They wanted to interject but what could they say with Ted present.

Max spoke up. "You're retiring?"

"I'm not retiring, but I'm not going to live forever. I will continue on as Founding Pastor."

Ted stared at his father, wondering where this new-found vote of confidence came from and why now. For years he waited in the wings, believing that if his father just put his full confidence behind him, he would have a shot at the church embracing him. Slowly, Ted allowed himself to entertain the notion that this was really happening, that he had finally won his father's confidence.

"We're very happy for you," Alexis said, leading the staff in offering obligatory congratulations. As she clapped, the rest of the room joined in.

"Well, at least the announcements are out of the way," Max interjected to break the awkwardness of the moment.

"Actually, I have one more," Reagan said.

As if on cue, Clay appeared in the doorway holding the coffee cake, hair tousled, twigs on his shirt and his pants dirt stained. He felt like a late party guest unsure if he had read the invitation correctly.

"Everyone…this is my other announcement. I have hired this young man to work for us on special projects."

Max and Alexis stared at each other. Had Reagan lost his mind? If the first announcement didn't send the staff over the top, this one certainly did. They may have had to contain their feelings about Ted, but not this.

"I can come back," Clay said, feeling the chilly reception.

"Forgive us, but your arrival is a surprise given the current budget constraints," Alexis said.

"Now Alexis, he did bring the coffee cake," Max smirked.

"Alexis is the director of women's ministries," Reagan said. "And Max is our illustrious executive pastor. He basically runs the place."

"Don't let him fool you, Reagan runs the show around here," Max clarified.

Reagan went around the room, introducing everyone by name. "And this is my son Ted."

Ted was as surprised as the rest of the staff. If he was really the new senior pastor, why hadn't his father at least consulted him on this new hire? "Welcome to our church," Ted said with hesitance. He couldn't place it, but there was something familiar about this guy.

"Are you from the Bay area?" Max inquired.

"Clayton comes to us from Massachusetts," Reagan

said, resembling a publicist.

"What part?"

"North of Boston," Clay answered.

"Thomas went to college in Boston," Reagan subtly warned Clay.

"Did you go to seminary there?" Max turned to Thomas. "What's the name of that place?"

"Gordon-Conwell."

"Yeah, did you go there?" Max asked again.

"No, I didn't." Clay was increasingly uncomfortable.

Ted stared at the guy, trying to figure out who he reminded him of.

"This position doesn't require seminary training," Reagan announced.

"You were working for a church, right?" Max assumed.

"Well, yeah, um…"

Alexis interjected, turning her attention back to Reagan. "I understand that you're grieving, but I just don't understand how you could do this without consulting any of us? We have nine positions without funding…nine.

"The wonderful thing about Alexis is that you never have to say 'I wonder what she meant by that?'" Reagan put his hand on Clay's shoulder. "I find it refreshing… really."

"I'm not questioning your leadership. I'm just saying… and I think I speak for everyone, this is irresponsible. We are already stretched too thin."

"Why don't you wait in Ted's office until we finish up

here?" Reagan suggested to Clay, finally relieving him of the tray of coffee cake. "It's just down the hall on the left."

Just as Clay turned to leave, Ted asked him one last question. "I didn't get your last name."

"My last name...?" Clay hesitated just long enough for Reagan to step in.

"Ironside...Clay Ironside."

Forcing a nervous smile, Clay heard the reverberation of cannon balls bursting in his head.

Chapter Seventeen

Clay sat restless in a chair, fingers tapping on the desk. He had that awful feeling he used to get whenever he'd be summoned to a studio executive's office. And that never ended well. Sometimes it was to inform him that there was a change in plans, always something he never had control over — like writing his best friend off the show. More often it was to clarify expectations and why he was the suddenly the root of the problem at hand. As a kid, he didn't know any better. He'd just sit there and take it. He glanced around the room. It was neat and organized, like Ted himself. Every book and pencil was in its proper place. He knew if it were his office, he would turn the desk around so it faced the window. Why face a hallway when you could look out over that landscape?

His eye caught a glimpse of a picture in a silver frame on Ted's desk. *Probably their Christmas card.* It was of Ted, his wife and son, a happy family. He picked it up thinking about Tyler from the night before.

"That was taken on Founder's Day."

Clay looked up, realizing that Ted had stepped into the office.

"It was all we could do to get my son to sit still long enough to take the picture." Ted smiled, shaking his head as he moved behind his desk. "He's a handful."

Clay glanced at the photograph again before placing the frame back on the desk. "I'm sorry about your mother's passing."

Ted stared out the window. "I'm managing, but my father has hardly been himself."

Clay turned his head, keeping an eye on the door. "Where is your father?"

"I don't know," Ted said with sarcasm. "He slipped out of staff meeting before I could speak with him."

"Maybe I'll wait back in the loft?" Clay nervously rose from the chair.

"Look, I know who you are." Ted stared right at him. "You look different, but you haven't changed."

Clay sunk back into his seat, knowing this was going to get ugly.

"What are you doing here? This is a church not a hideout."

"Hey, this was your father's idea, not mine."

"My father is a visionary — thinks outside the box —

sometimes too outside the box." Ted had just won his father's confidence. He wasn't about to jeopardize the church. "It's not right for you to bring your mess here."

"You need to talk to him about this." Clay stood up to leave.

"Why him...?" Ted's face was red and his voice was getting louder. "Of all the people in the world, what made you track down my father after all these years?"

Clay wasn't twelve anymore and wasn't about to take much more. "I told you, you need to talk to him about this."

"My mother dies, and you show up on his doorstep? Don't you have a conscience?"

"He tracked me down."

"That's impossible. When would he have...?" Ted's eyes widened. Slowly, he realized what his father had done. Ted felt the abandonment all over again. His relationship with his father was just one more thing he tried to hold together that had long since been broken.

"He showed up in Boston a few days ago. Before I knew it, he had spoken to the judge and worked out a deal to pay off my debt. I didn't ask for a dime. He did that all on his own."

"We're paying off your debt?"

"The deal is that I would work it off."

"Doing what? What could you possibly do here to pay that off? From what I heard on TV, that's a big debt. How long are you planning on being here?"

"I don't know. Everything's happened pretty fast. I just

figured that stuff would work itself out."

"Here's some free advice, before you enter into a deal with my father, it's always a good idea to look closely at the terms."

Clay and Ted realized that Tyler was standing in the doorway. He was covered in dirt with a note pinned to his shirt. Tyler recognized Clay from the night before. "Are you in trouble too?"

"Oh, yeah…"

Ted realized that they knew each other. He unpinned the note and glanced over it. "Wait here! I'll deal with you later. I have to talk to your grandfather right now."

Tyler let out an impressive laugh once his father stepped out of the office. "Whatever you did, it must have been big."

"Does your dad always get that worked up?"

"He's been worse since my mom left for grad school." Tyler made a fist and punched Clay in the arm. "Don't worry about it."

Clay slouched in his chair.

"Are you hungry?"

Clay's eyes widened. "Starving. I didn't even get any coffee cake."

"Follow me." Tyler offered a mischievous smile.

Clay followed Tyler through the corridor and down the back stairs. As they made their way outside the administration building, Tyler made sure that the coast was clear before cutting across the expansive lawn.

"Come on." Tyler darted ahead and took cover behind a protective tree.

Clay tried to keep up. Catching his breath, he turned his head and looked back. Through a vast tree branch, he could see a view of Reagan's office window. He could tell that Reagan was trying to calm Ted down. Both were engaged, standing face-to-face. After a moment of the heated exchange, he could see Ted turn away from his father and then Reagan putting his hand on Ted's shoulder. Clay knew this was the beginning of the end.

"Are you coming or not?" Tyler called out, reaching for the asthma inhaler in his pocket.

Clay took a last look at the window and then continued on.

* * *

The church kitchen was a heavily guarded fortress. Not only did it have a security camera outside, but because of it's proximity to Friendship Courtyard, it was virtually impossible to enter without being noticed. The only other way in, though quite unlikely, was through the service window in Celebration Hall, but even then the intruder would have to have stolen a key to the service window and then have been small enough to slip through before opening the swinging door to any accomplices. This unlikely scenario was quickly dismissed by the staff, but mysterious food raids continued to baffle them.

"Are you sure we're allowed in here?" Clay said.

Tyler's feet dangled in the air as he squeezed through the opening. "You worry too much."

"I just don't want to get you into trouble."

"I'm a PK. I'm supposed to get into trouble."

"What's a PK?" Clay heard a loud thump as Tyler landed in the kitchen.

"A preacher's kid…" Tyler rumbled through the kitchen, bumping into pots and pans. "I got a reputation to live up to." And as easy as that, the door swung open.

The inside of the kitchen smelled like ice burn and Orange Tang. Black rubber mats covered the floor, while stainless steel refrigerators, complete with padlocks, lined the walls.

Clay smirked as Tyler removed a key ring from his pocket and began trying various keys. This kid was too much. After a moment, the locks started popping open.

"Jackpot!"

With all this security, Clay half expected to discover the Arc of the Covenant — or at the least a fatted calf chained inside. He rolled his eyes. He just couldn't imagine what sacred grub was worth protecting until visions of Prosciutto and Prime Rib began dancing in his head. His stomach growled as he waited in anticipation.

One by one, the three refrigerators opened. "What will it be?"

Clay's hopeful eyes scanned the shelves. The multitude of leftovers sat in aluminum containers covered in plastic wrap. It looked like the day after Thanksgiving…actually, the day, after the day, after the day of Thanksgiving. Each tray was clearly labeled with a ministry name followed by an ominous warning that read: "Do Not Touch."

Tyler read off the labels as if they were the specials of

the day. "…Left-over pasta salad from the women's ministry, a few turkey burgers from the singles' ministry social, maybe flank steak from the college ministry's outreach…?"

Clay was overwhelmed by the culinary selection, although he had yet to see anything that merited being kept under lock and key.

"And if you don't like any of that…" Tyler unlocked the walk-in freezer. "There is always the High Hope favorite…PriceSmart Lasagna!"

Frost poured out as he opened the industrial door. It was shelf after shelf of PriceSmart Lasagna. There were probably fifty trays.

"That's a lot of lasagna," Clay said over the roaring hum of the freezer fan. "Is it any good?"

Tyler stared at Clay in disbelief. "You've never had PriceSmart Lasagna?"

Clay shook his head "no," somehow embarrassed by the admission.

"Sorry. I just assumed you were a Christian."

Clay smirked. "What does PriceSmart Lasagna have to do with being a Christian?"

"Are you kidding, me? It's like the official food of Christianity. It's the cheapest, easiest thing to serve. It's as common to church life as miniature golf, bowling, or renting *The Princess Bride*."

"*The Princess Bride*…?"

"No dirty language or naked people." Tyler closed the freezer door. "You can't imagine how much PriceSmart

Lasagna a Christian eats a year!"

"But is it any good?"

Tyler stopped in his tracks having never considered the question. "It's the only lasagna I know."

"That's one of the saddest things I've ever heard."

"So what will it be?" Tyler started removing trays from the refrigerators. "Personally, I'd take the flank steak."

Conviction came over Clay. As hungry as he was, he couldn't get past the "Do Not Touch" labels.

"We can't eat this. It's like stealing." Clay pointed to the names on the labels. "This food belongs to these ministries."

Tyler rolled his persuasive blue eyes; obviously Clay was only familiar with literal interpretations of the Bible. "And what are ministries supposed to do?"

For the life of him, Clay couldn't muster up an answer.

"Feed the poor! I don't know about you, but I'm broke."

Clay smirked as the miniature theologian removed the flank steak and placed it on the center counter top.

"Wait until dessert," Tyler said with excitement. "Alcoholics Anonymous makes killer oatmeal cookies!"

They sat on the stainless steel counter top, which was covered with leftovers and open containers. Clay finished off another bowl of chili while Tyler munched on his fourth oatmeal cookie. They had pieced together a feast from all the scraps and the food coma was setting in.

"So what's so terrible about being a 'PK'?"

"Are you kidding, me? It's the worst." Tyler chewed on

the cookie. "People are always coming up to me, pinching my cheeks, telling me how cute I am. I hate that."

Clay scraped the bottom of the bowl with his spoon. "I wasn't a 'PK,' but I can relate. By the time I was your age, I had no feeling left in my cheeks."

"And that's not the worst part. I have to be involved with everything. People are always staring at me. It's like they are waiting for me to mess up."

"Tell me about it." Clay licked the spoon recalling his own youthful plight.

"You have no idea."

"Oh, you'd be surprised."

"And when I do get into trouble, the whole church knows about it. The whole church! Then everybody is either giving you advice or telling you how lucky you are." Tyler took a last look at the half-eaten cookie and then tossed it back on the counter. "I don't feel lucky."

"That stinks." If anyone could feel for the kid, it was Clay.

"My mom is always reminding dad and grandpa that I'm not 'church property.'"

"But your dad was a 'PK'?"

"Grandpa says he's still waiting for dad to mess up."

"Trust me you're better off not listening to what people say about you, good or bad."

"I get that."

"You do?" Clay was unprepared for what he was about to hear.

"People project onto me their own desire for moral

perfection," Tyler said nonchalantly. "An unrealistic expectation I can't live up to. Ultimately, I mess up and they're disappointed."

Clay shot Tyler a "did you just say that?" look.

"At least that's what my therapist says."

"Therapist...? What are you, nine?"

"I'm a 'PK.' The sooner the better." Just as Tyler resigned himself to his fate, Diego entered the kitchen.

"Busted..."

Tyler froze as he realized that Diego was in the doorway. He knew he was in trouble and that he couldn't outrun Diego.

Hopping off the counter, Clay attempted to take the blame. "It's my fault, really. I was hungry, and the kid was just trying to help me out."

Diego smiled at Clay. "Nice try." He held out his hand in front of Tyler. "All right...hand them over."

Tyler reluctantly reached into his pocket, pulling out Diego's key ring.

"You're getting too good at swiping these."

Clay made an appeal to Diego, trying to protect Tyler. "Is there any way we could prevent the kid from getting into trouble?"

"Don't worry about it." Diego glanced at Tyler. "This time!"

Tyler smirked. "You haven't told on me yet."

"The key word is 'yet.' Now clean this up!"

Tyler hopped off the counter and began wiping the counter, putting containers in the trash. He resembled a miniature custodian.

Diego turned to Clay. "Reagan's looking for you."

Clay rolled his eyes. He knew what that meant. He was convinced he was going to break the deal. He hadn't been here twenty-four hours and the place was already turned upside down. That was almost a personal record.

Following Diego outside the kitchen, they stopped in front of Friendship Courtyard.

Clay squinted from the sharp sunlight. "That's cool, the way you look out for Tyler."

"He's a good kid. Just has a lot of pressure on him."

"His mom isn't coming back, is she?"

Diego shook his head, no.

After an awkward moment, Diego noticed that Clay looked a bit pale. "Man, you don't look so good."

Clay rubbed his stomach. "I just ate my weight in leftover chili from Volunteer Appreciation Day."

"Volunteer Appreciation Day…? That was like six weeks ago."

Clay looked like he was going to be sick. "Tyler!"

Diego patted him on the back as they continued to walk. "Crime doesn't pay, my friend. Crime doesn't pay."

Ted stood in the pulpit, practicing his sermon to an empty sanctuary. His tone and animated gestures were forced. Each time he said "Juanita Gonzalez" he used a Hispanic accent.

"You see Juanita Gonzalez had a fuel problem. But not the kind of fuel you're probably thinking of."

The next line fell flat. "Juanita Gonzalez was low not on food or gasoline, but faith." Ted tried again, this time using a signature Bill Clinton hand gesture — making a fist while pointing with his thumb. "Juanita Gonzalez was low not on food or gasoline," he paused, "but faith."

Reagan and Clay settled into the dusty theater seats in the balcony loft, secretly observing Ted's performance. They spoke in a quiet whisper so as not to be noticed.

"He's been over-coached. That's my fault."

Clay was certain of one thing: If there really was a Juanita Gonzalez, Ted didn't know her. It sounded like one of those contrived campaign stories politicians tell to show that they're connected with the people. Clay learned early on to never underestimate your audience. They can see right through it. Glancing at Reagan, he only wished he had been that perceptive. Like a fool, Clay had underestimated Reagan's ability to stick by him. What did he expect? Blood was thicker than water. Shifting uncomfortably in his seat, he waited for Reagan's rationale of why he was going to break the deal.

"I spoke to my generation. I had hoped that Ted could speak to his. This isn't inspiring you, is it?"

Normally, Clay would show some restraint, but at this point he had nothing to lose. "Is the real problem the message or the man?"

"I always believed that the right words could change the man."

"Well these aren't them. Not that I go to church, but

if I had to sit through this every week, I don't think I'd ever come back."

"I agree…"

Clay was surprised by the admission.

"And that is why I've decided that the church is never going to hear it."

"What?"

"I've obtained someone to write it for him."

Clay smirked, familiar with the nameless writers who would come in to punch up a script. He felt foolish thinking Reagan was above such practices. He whispered back, "I hope he's good."

"I'm betting on it. In fact I've bet a great deal on it." Reagan turned to Clay and smiled.

"You got to be kidding me. You brought me all the way here for this?" Clay felt the adrenaline race through his body. "I'm not a pastor."

"Good…we have plenty of them."

"I don't write anymore, let alone anything that sounds like a sermon."

"Not a sermon, a message. It doesn't have to be long. Just share a word that will resonate with the people — something that you would want to hear from the pulpit."

"This is insane. Besides it's dishonest."

"Dishonest?" Reagan reached into his pocket and removed a crumpled paper. "I also spent some time with your lawyer when I was in Boston. It seems that he didn't write that compelling argument that impressed the judge after all. You wrote it."

Clay stared at that crumpled paper filled with his own handwriting.

"What is needed is the humanity of someone who has been broken, someone like you."

Clay realized that Reagan was serious. Eyes rising, he stared at the jagged crack that skirted the central beam in the balcony ceiling overhead.

"God has given you a gift with words. I'd rather you try and fail than sit on the sidelines. You've sat on the sidelines too long. Besides, the church won't receive his words, but they might receive yours."

* * *

Thunder rattled the windows of the motel lobby, the steady downpour beating against the glass. Burt waited for the airport shuttle.

Gossip magazines with headlines about Clay littered the counter. Burt tucked a few in his bag. He couldn't wait to get out of Boston. *How the hell does someone disappear without leaving a trail?* He entered his credit card into the airline website, booking a ticket to the one person he was sure could point him in the right direction.

Glancing out the rain soaked window, he spotted newspapers for sale covering the story. The first picture of Clay now could fetch up to six hundred thousand. There was no way he was going to let someone else profit from this kid. The shuttle bus pulled up. Printing out his receipt, he knew exactly where he was headed.

Chapter Eighteen

His first instinct was to run. As he returned to the loft to pack, he plotted his escape along the way. He'd borrow Diego's truck to get down the mountain, making sure to let him know where it was once he was out of sight. He knew he'd have to lay low for a while. The Cal Trans station in Daly City was probably his best bet. He had spotted it from the highway on the drive in. He could catch a train or bus there. He wouldn't care where it was headed as long as it was away from here. He felt manipulated. He knew he had every right to run. And that was exactly what he planned to do when he entered the loft. So why did his bags remain empty on the hardwood floor?

Lying on the bed, he stared at the ceiling, his thoughts churning. He couldn't understand it. What would make Reagan think he could write the message? He thought about that crumpled piece of paper. He had stayed up half the night writing it, his ink-stained fingers cramping as he articulated a defense he had played out in his mind a thousand times before. In the end, it wasn't enough. He couldn't get past it. He had watched his lawyer throw it in the trash. So much of his heart had been poured into those words that it was as if a piece of him was being discarded, another fragment out there that he'd never get back. His eyes filled with water.

The idea that Reagan had retrieved it overwhelmed him. Clay couldn't bring himself to run out on the man, at least not yet.

There had to be another way. And then the idea came to him. He got up from the bed and moved to the window. He spotted the flowing stream at the base of the hill. Maybe it wasn't such a crazy idea after all?

Ted was at risk, not him. What was the worst that could happen? If it was a disaster, they'd send him packing anyhow. Ted would insist on it. He wouldn't screw up on purpose, but the odds were in his favor. He didn't have to run out on Reagan. All he had to do was come up with something that let Reagan know he tried. Staring at that bubbling creek, he wondered if he could find the words.

Clay walked across campus. He wasn't running, he was walking. There was difference.

He couldn't believe that he was actually considering

writing it. Or that a part of him was flattered — the boy inside of him that was never heard. As a kid it was a constant battle. As a teenager, it was just outright rebellion. He didn't have a say in anything. Even his interviews were well scripted. It was ironic: now that someone wanted to hear what he had to say, it would be said through someone else.

He thought about what Reagan said about the right words changing the man. All Clay knew were the words that had changed him, the accusing comments that kept him in line and replayed in his head. He prided himself on not caring what other people thought or said, but if he was honest, he knew that stuff lingered and had a way of resurfacing, especially when he was tired and alone. The wrong words stay with you a lot longer than the right ones. He wouldn't say it, but that was what he believed.

Continuing toward the center of campus, he took in the quiet majesty of the landscape. It was beautiful. He had to admit that was one promise Reagan came through on. That and the bad reception....

He thought about what he wanted to hear from the pulpit. He smirked. Even if he could imagine what he would want to hear, he was certain it wasn't fit for public airing. One thing was certain, he thought as he continued down the hill, if he had any shot at helping Ted, he would have to keep all his private thoughts about the realities of life to himself.

* * *

Alexis confronted Reagan as they made their way down the church corridor. Their conversation was as intense as their pace. Not wanting to be overheard, they spoke in a quiet tone.

"Resigning...?" Reagan said.

"You still have time to change this."

"Names... I need names."

Alexis was reluctant. As a therapist, she respected confidentiality, but as a co-worker, her instinct was to prevent a mass exodus. "Paul... Monica..."

Reagan didn't flinch. He expected casualties. "Is that it?"

Alexis hesitated before breaking the news. "And Max."

"Max...?" Reagan was clearly disappointed. Every church has a leader that the people follow regardless of title or position. At High Hope, that was Max. In fact, in the three years he had been there young families began returning to the church for the first time in more than a decade. "We can't afford to lose him."

"They've been sitting on offers for weeks. Ted and this new hire... they were the deciding factor."

They passed Monica Wilson in the corridor.

"Great staff meeting, Reagan. Very inspiring!" She held a thumb up to emphasis the point.

"Thank you for your belief, Monica." Reagan offered a confident grin as Monica moved down the corridor. "Offers from where...?"

"Monica's going to Harvey Maxwell's church in Florida,

and Paul…he's leaving the ministry. He was offered a job at Oracle."

"Oracle…?" They stepped into Reagan's office. "It's one thing to lose a pastor to Harvey Maxwell, but to Larry Ellison?"

Alexis tried to explain. "His kids are almost in college. He thinks he can make good money."

"And Max?"

"Pearl Tree Pond…"

Reagan shook his head in disappointment.

"That's where he went last month when he took those personal days," Alexis said. "I know their offer will be hard to beat."

"They're not going to let him preach in the main service?"

"Maybe the Sunday after Christmas…that sort of thing…"

"Max won't survive one winter in Chicago," Reagan said.

"You are betting everything on this…everything on Ted and Mr. Ironside."

* * *

As Clay came down the hill, he stumbled upon the High Hope Bookstore situated in Friendship Courtyard next to a vending cart that sold coffee and pastries. He hoped they would have what he was looking for.

The bookstore was really more of a gift shop than anything else, filled with keepsakes and collectibles. There were separate teen and children's sections and a special counter where you could buy sermons from the previous weeks. Although you could get most of what they had online, people still preferred to come into the store; the inspirational atmosphere was invigorating and made people feel as if they were embodying Reagan's message of hope. All this was especially true since word got out about Rose. It had been busy all week, but the store had yet to extend its hours. It was pretty much cleaned out. Anything with a High Hope logo went fast. Everyone, it seemed, wanted a piece of Hope.

The volunteers were anxious to ring up the last of the customers and close up shop by three. Bessie and Grace were sisters and knew if they hurried, they were usually able to catch the hourglass opening of their favorite soap opera on the black-and-white television set in the backroom. Although the reception was poor, the iconic theme was stirring enough to make them feel like they were listening to an old radio broadcast. If they missed the theme, they were never quite able to get into the rest of the show and would instead focus on the poor picture quality and unrealistic storylines.

So at a quarter to three, the sisters began giving subtle hints to the customers that they were closing — like turning off the soaring Praise Music and shutting down the rotating display cases. In fact, the closer it came to the three o'clock hour, the less inspiring everything seemed.

Needless to say, they were none-too-happy when Clay wandered in while everyone else was checking out. He noticed their anxious smiles, but was quickly distracted by the picked-over inspirational products scattered throughout. He was confident that if he got inside Ted's audiences' mind, he could bust out something that was at least better than Ted's 'Juanita Gonzalez' message.

His eyes rose to the artwork for sale on the walls. There were scenes of quaint cottages with thatched roofs nestled in tranquil valleys, framed with comforting scriptures about peace and serenity. They weren't originals. They were "hand-numbered" prints that had been, according to the nearby sign, "individually highlighted by trained apprentices under the supervision of the artist." Clay stared at the cottages, curious who lived inside. He half-expected one of the three little pigs to come wandering out.

Making his way to the back of the store, he perused the book section. It was largely a monument to Reagan, his thirty titles proudly displayed. He picked up one and flipped through the pages, his eyes fixated on the motivational sayings that were highlighted in bold text. They seemed more inspirational than theological, the sum of which was sort of a roadmap to a better life. It occurred to Clay that you didn't even need to read it; if you read the headings, you pretty much read the book. In fact, the title alongside Reagan's confident face was probably enough to lift your spirits if this was the sort of thing you bought into.

Maybe this stuff did work, as long as you lived in one

of those quaint, thatched-roofed cottages in one of those villages featured in the paintings. And just as long as the mortgage was paid and the creditors weren't calling and you hadn't been informed that the government was going to build a new freeway through your front yard. Yeah, then this stuff might work.

But the only valleys he had known were anything but tranquil. Pits, really, that were steep and incredibly hard to climb out of. He wasn't one for positive sentiments, the kind that disappear the moment you wander from your safe cottage, given you live in one in the first place. Even if he was just being cynical, he knew better than to lift his hopes that high.

He stared at the book in his hand again. If this is what the audience wanted, he was uncertain he could deliver. Besides, there was only one Reagan. Reagan could get away with this stuff, but not Ted.

Just when he felt that the situation was looking dim, the lights went out.

Bessie stood by the switch, smiling. It was the last of her not-so-subtle hints that it was closing time.

Message received. Tossing the book back onto the pile, he turned to leave. It was then that he encountered Jesus, well sort of. His path was blocked by Grace who held open an oversized "Jesus is my Shepherd" afghan to fold. Clay was taken aback at the sight of the overly-friendly Savior in colorful woven thread towering over him.

Pivoting away, he inadvertently backed into a display table of "Jesus" consumer products and knocked them over: Biblical action figures, Last Supper platters, "Jesus and the Boyz" t-shirts and several "Lamp unto my feet" night lights. They tumbled off the shelves, the tinny noise of the "Last Supper" platters echoing as they hit the ground.

Bessie and Grace watched in dismay, their anxious smiles turning into frowns as all hope for their favorite soap opera quickly faded.

Clay attempted to pick up the items that were scattered about, recalling a time when his face was plastered on cheap merchandise. He wondered if Jesus felt the same way. He stared knowingly at the muscle-clad Jesus action figure in his hand.

"Bad licensing deals, huh? I know all about that."

* * *

Max stepped into Reagan's office. He was wearing Thomas' sport coat over his golfing attire. "Alexis said you wanted to see me?"

Reagan offered Max a seat. "My afternoon is packed, so I'll make this fast. As I see it, you have a problem on your hands."

"I have a problem?" Max grinned, curious where this was going.

Reagan reached into his desk and removed a golf ball. He held it between his thumb and index finger. "Maybe you've forgotten, but golf balls are white."

Max stared at the ball confused. "I don't follow."

"Golf balls are white. Unfortunately, so are golf courses…in Chicago. Not green. White. How are you going to see the white ball if the course is covered in snow?" Reagan tossed the ball to Max.

"Alexis told you…."

"Look, we both know that the point of any game is to never take your eye off the ball. I'm afraid that is exactly what you are doing."

"Ted is a good man, but he's not you. Right or wrong, you're the reason people come week after week. You're the draw."

"I'm not disappearing. I'm just giving Ted an opportunity."

"I have to look out for my family. If this place unravels—"

"You're not leaving."

Max let out a chuckle. "I admit it…Reagan Mitchell can motivate anyone to do just about anything. But not me…. Not this time."

"Paul and Monica are leaving," Reagan admitted.

"I know…."

"I won't try to stop them," Reagan said. "I know their hearts left long ago. But not yours. Your heart is in the soil of this church."

"Don't do this."

"Think of all the families that are invested here because of you. They're still young in their faith. You're going to walk out on them now?"

Max gripped the golf ball tighter.

"Pearl Street Pond is a turn-key operation. You'll never be able to do there what you can accomplish here." Reagan made a final appeal. "Don't take your eye off the ball, not now."

Chapter Nineteen

Clay made his way into town along Ridge Road, kicking
up dirt with each step as he descended the tree-lined
hill. He had heard of determined men walking across the
country on foot, but until this moment, he had never fully
understood it. If not for the media aattention it would
surely attract, or what lay on the other side of the country
for him—namely Boston—he might have kept walking.

He felt caught between what had been stirred up
inside of him and the danger that lay further down the
mountain. It had been a heavy news cycle, but by now
the mainstream media would be all over the story. Burt
would be more determined than ever, wanting to profit
from the story before the paparazzi did. The outside world
wasn't safe, and yet something about seeing all those
cheap consumer products made him want to flee.

Slowing his pace, he approached the quaint town telling himself to calm down and to shake it off. But that was easier said than done. Memories could be as powerful as the words that accompanied them, both capable of erasing the distance time had put in place.

Rounding the Acorn Diner, he stepped from the dirt road onto the steady pavement of Cliff Falls Drive. He glanced in the window, hoping a glimpse of Becky might brighten his day. Instead he spotted Ted sitting at the counter. Cringing, he stepped away from the glass before Ted could see him, curious what language could make this guy appealing. Ted was not worth the aggravation, but Clay knew he didn't have much of a choice. He had to buy time until things blew over. Besides he wasn't doing this for Ted. He was doing it for Reagan.

Continuing down the street, he passed the various storefronts of the picture perfect town — Nancy's Knitting Shop, Cliff Falls Hardware Store, The Perfect Note Stationery and Gift Shop. He felt foolish getting so worked up, but didn't think he should have to feel that junk again just to please an audience. He hated being in that position.

He hesitated in front of the fire house. Why was he making this so difficult? *Keep it simple. Show you tried. That will buy you time until things settle down and allow you to save face with Reagan.* That's what he reminded himself as he stood in the town square, hoping that his bare minimum would be enough. Now if he could just figure out how to write something that pleased the High Hope audience and didn't make Clay stir up bad memories, he'd be a happy man.

Noticing a crossing guard escorting children across the busy intersection, he got an idea.

Clay walked into the children's section of the Cliff Falls library and approached the reference librarian. Here was the perfect compromise. Everyone respected children's literature. All he had to do was quote a few books and write something akin to a graduation speech with a faith message tacked on the end. After all, most of what High Hope was used to was inspirational anyhow. In fact, Ted would be better served if Clay could just make him more likeable. If he did that, he would have accomplished a great task.

He noticed a few parents quietly reading to their children as the librarian helped him gather the titles he requested. Most of the books, he was embarrassed to admit, he hadn't begun reading until he was well into his twenties. He reasoned that while some adults revisited their childhood in their twenties and thirties, others were just trying to discover it.

He sat at a children's table, his adult body crammed into the miniature plastic chair. The stack of classics covered the tabletop: *Charlotte's Web*, *The Giving Tree*, *The Outsiders*, and his personal favorite, *The Little Prince*. He transferred a memorable quote onto the back of a library index card with a crayon.

"All grown-ups were children first. (But few remember it)."

He marinated in the truth of the statement, although he personally knew a few adults he had suspected were never children. But that was beside the point. He had enough content in these books to compose something that at least showed he tried. No one could ask more than that.

"Tell me you're not going to use *The Little Prince*! Everyone quotes *The Little Prince*!"

Clay looked up and discovered the blond mop top standing beside him.

"You're going to have to come up with something better than that if you're going to help my dad."

"How…what…?"

"I was in the back of the balcony when you were talking to my grandfather."

Clay raised his eyebrows. This kid was too much.

Tyler sorted through the other books on the table. "*Oh, the Places You'll Go*! You got to be kidding? Original…we need something original here!"

"Maybe you should help him?" Clay shot back.

"Shhhhh…" The librarian placed her finger over her lips. They quieted down.

Clay recognized the silent anxiety in Tyler's eyes, a burden too heavy for any kid his age. He put down his crayon. "Why are you worried about all this, really?"

Tyler hesitated, but knew he could trust him. "If my dad does a good job…my mom might transfer to Stanford."

"Did she tell you that?"

"I just think—"

"Tyler, it doesn't work that way. This is adult stuff. Your parents have to work it out for themselves."

But Tyler didn't want to hear it. He was convinced that he could fix anything with a little help. He held out his pinkie finger. "Just promise me that you'll make my dad look good."

Clay stared at the boy with bewilderment.

"Promise...."

Chapter Twenty

The typist entered "Clay Grant" into the Google search engine. 750,000 results appeared including:

"Mysterious Backlot Fire"
"LGM Sightings"
"Little Guy – Big Tax Debt"
"LGM: Dead or Alive – Urban Legends"
"CLAYHEART Auctions – *Little Guy Mike* Memorabilia"

Click. The EBAY page opened revealing dozens of *Little Guy Mike* items up for auction as the page scrolled down. Bidding wars were in progress. Lots were cast for many of the same consumer products once destroyed by Clay, each listing with a colorful snapshot, current bid, and time remaining.

"LGM Lunch Box and Thermos"
$149   17h   43m
"Autographed 8 by 10 headshot of Clay"
$77   1d   12h   19m
"A 'Little Guy Mike' Halloween mask"
$219   2d   14h   32m
"A TV Guide featuring Clay on the cover"
$135   3d   8h   11m

Click. The "Little Guy Mike" Halloween mask appeared on screen. It was a rare item and was in decent condition.

Ted stared at the happy plastic face with rosy cheeks, tempted to bid on the lot. He couldn't believe how popular the guy still was and what people were willing to pay for a piece of him. Whoever was running this site was making bank.

Ted glanced out his office window. What was his father thinking bringing this trouble here?

* * *

Clay woke up early the next morning. Curling up in the blanket, he felt safe enough to sleep. It was amazing, he never realized how exhausted he was until he stopped running. But by afternoon he still hadn't written a word. Sitting on the woven oval rug on the floor of his loft apartment, he was already regretting the promise he made to Tyler. He knew the power of a pinkie swear was a binding contract. What was he thinking, especially after breaking his promise to Bella? He didn't want to lie, but he also didn't want to crush the boy's hope.

Reaching into his pocket, he looked over the list of instructions Tyler gave him, including what movie references not to use.

"No *Braveheart*, no *Matrix*, and especially no *Chariots of Fire*!"

Somehow the bar had just been raised. He couldn't care less about Ted, but that kid was another story.

"I had forgotten how peaceful this loft was…"

Clay looked up and realized Reagan was standing in the doorway.

"As a young pastor, I wrote all my sermons here…. I used to lock myself up here for days…writing at that desk…gazing out that window. This was the one place I could always escape to…even if just for a little while."

Clay started to get up but Reagan motioned him not to bother. "I can't stay long."

Clenching Tyler's list in his hand, Clay understood more was at stake than even Reagan realized.

"I don't want to screw this up for you. Get someone else. I'm sure you know people."

Reagan didn't want to hear it. "If you're having trouble writing, just dig deeper…."

Obviously, this man's grief had affected his judgment. But Clay realized that trying to convince him otherwise was no use.

Reagan turned to leave, glancing at the loft. "Rose was right. I never should have stopped writing here."

As Reagan left, Clay glanced again at the paper in his hand. Getting up, he went to the window. Looking out, he was once more mesmerized by the bubbling creek at the base of the hill. He thought about searching for the elusive falls, but figured he was lost enough as it was. What he really needed to do was clear his head.

Wandering down by the bubbling brook at the base of the hillside, he felt rested, thousands of miles away from civilization and from anyone who could hurt him. Putting his hand in the trickling water, he'd like to believe that the stream really did originate from the falls everyone talked about.

Why did it always feel like the weight of everyone else's lives was always on his shoulders?

Clay was twelve when he first realized that all the people pleasing in the world would never make them love him or make his mom come back.

Beads of sweat dripped down his forehead, melting the pancake makeup on his face. Throat dry, he couldn't speak. He could feel them all around him, staring from the rafters, from the wings and from behind the camera, waiting, every eye on him. All their jobs rested on how he delivered his lines.

The show was struggling to find its audience. Network was thinking of pulling the plug. One executive said a game show would do better at 8:00 PM on a Tuesday night and would be cheaper to produce.

The week before, his friend's series got canceled after five years, having read about it in the trades. Now the guy wasn't even allowed on the lot. When the kid and his mom came back the next afternoon to clean out his dressing room they were turned away at the security gate by the same guy who greeted them everyday for the past five years.

It felt like a family, and everyone said it was, but it wasn't one, not really.

He delivered the catch phrase and all he heard was laughter. Everyone in the wings and everyone on the rafters were smiling. He knew he would have to make that happen every time.

He had come out here to clear his head. Why did all these memories keep coming back to him? Clay shook the water from his hands, stood up, and moved on.

He traced the brook upstream hoping his memories would dissipate in the sound of bubbling water. No such luck.

Clay followed the weathered fence towards the north side of the property. He spotted a High Hope truck outside the old barn. It was about as beaten up as the barn itself.

The old barn was a shell of a structure. If not for it being the oldest building on the campus, it would have been knocked down years ago.

Clay pulled the door back, the hinges creaking from the effort. He stepped into the barn and was suddenly awestruck by what he discovered.

The golden beams poured in from the rafters through cracks in the shingled roof, illuminating the canvasses that littered the barn.

The paintings hung on rusty hooks nailed to the timber, their violent purple and red strokes contrasting with the decaying wood that surrounded them. Each captured a moment on a sorrowful path, the progression of a contorted body and injured flesh. There must have been a dozen.

Clay hesitated, feet planted in the dirt below, as the weary eyes cried out to him. He recognized the sequence. It was *The Way of the Cross*, a series of paintings depicting the final hours of Jesus' life.

The anguish of a twisted torso bloodied by the lashes of rage…the laughing faces of ridicule…a shoulder slumping under the pressure of the splintered beam, knees collapsing under the weight, falling to the ground …fingers pointed in judgment…lots cast for clothing… the mockery of a purple cloak….

The paintings provoked something more inside of him than other inspirational art he had seen. Perhaps it was the sum of the collection, that each moment had been memorialized, that each moment mattered. Or maybe it was that they were hidden within this weathered barn. All he knew was that he felt like he was stepping on sacred ground.

He moved forward as dust particles danced in the light, the hallowed paintings on either side of him drawing him in. It was as if he were taking part in the journey, a bystander in the crowd looking on.

With each step he was increasingly aware of the determined eyes as the rays continued to seep in through the fractured wood. For a moment he couldn't tell if the light was pouring in or pouring out.

An easel stood in the middle of the barn. It was a work-in-progress, the artist's jagged pencil sketch hidden by the seemingly random strokes of the brush.

Clay moved in closer. He could see the dripping paint, the colors bleeding, bubbling, attempting to dry from the light that bled through the fractured wood. He had seen other versions a thousand times before, but only now did he understand it: It was hope taking its last breath.

He would have stared at the canvas forever if he had not been interrupted.

"It's far from complete." Diego stood a few feet away holding a pail filled with turpentine and several brushes.

"You did all this?"

"Not all at once."

"They are amazing. Really, I wouldn't just say that. You should show them. Have an art show. Hang them in the sanctuary or something." Clay couldn't get over the vividness of the paintings or what they stirred in him.

"It just feels good to get paint on your hands." For Diego, creating for an audience of One was enough. Everything didn't need to be exploited, marketed or end up on a calendar or a Power Point slide.

"I'm telling you, these are beautiful…" Clay said.

"Have you ever considered what God created that will never be seen by human eyes, like fish in the depths of the sea? What He created just because that's what a creator does? I think about that all the time."

"Unfortunately, most of what I've created I wouldn't consider art."

"It's like a kid's painting…if your heart is in it, it's art."

Clay felt conviction stir up inside of him even though his heart wasn't part of the deal. He glanced at the paintings again and then back at Diego. "You know that old truck out front. Does it still run?"

"I think we can get her going."

Diego handed Clay keys to the weathered High Hope truck.

Climbing in, Clay felt the springs and coils in the seat. Turning the key, he started the engine. It sputtered, exhaust pouring out of the tailpipe.

"I'm assuming this didn't pass a smog check," Clay said over the engine's rumble.

"We plant a tree every time we take her out." Diego smiled.

Offering directions, Diego pointed down the dirt road. The truck pulled away.

The flashing neon sign out front read "The Dutch Goose." He was about eight miles from Hope, but it felt like the edge of civilization. Inside, the dimly lit room was crowded with a mix of Stanford students and technology professionals unwinding after work. The pool tables and peanuts seemed to be the main attraction.

Clay sat at the bar with a blank notepad, watching Sports Center, cracking and eating peanuts. Something about the barn had inspired him.

The pile of shells surrounding his portion of the counter grew as thoughts were written down and then promptly crossed out. It had been a while since he put his heart into anything.

"Can I get you another?" The bartender asked.

Clay looked up from writing. "How does this sound?" He read from the pad.

"It's one thing to believe in something when you don't need it to be true. It's another when everything is riding on it."

"Sounds like you've been eating too much Chinese food."

Clay crumpled up the paper figuring he'd have been better off with a bag of fortune cookies for inspiration.

"But don't take my word for it," the portly bartender backtracked. "I'm not very deep. At least that's what Tommy says. We should ask Tommy. Tommy's smart. Tommy has his Doctorate in philosophy. Hey Tommy, how does this sound?"

Tommy sat at the opposite end of the bar. He had a narrow beard and wore a t-shirt with a portrait of Rasputin. He responded with a reluctant, but curious gaze.

This was not exactly Clay's target audience, but he had nothing to lose. He reluctantly repeated the line. "It's one thing to believe in something when you don't need it to be true. It's another when everything is riding on it."

Clay and the bartender waited in silence as Tommy stared at them as if he had just tasted a foreign Merlot with unfamiliar characteristics. He seemed unwilling to either smile or spit it out. Clay would have preferred either reaction.

"Interesting…" Tommy said in a detached, analytical tone. "And by 'believe' you mean what exactly?"

Clay tried to explain. "How do you know what you *really* believe unless you have had to rely on it? Unless something was at stake?"

"Interesting…" he said again in the same non-committal tone, somehow incapable of emoting. "And by 'rely,' you mean what exactly?"

All Clay could think was if Tommy went to Stanford, he should get his money back. "That's all right, really. If I have to explain it, it's probably not working…."

Clay crossed out the line and returned his attention to the peanuts and Sports Center.

After a few moments an attractive woman smiled at him. However, he was more interested in the peanuts. Finally she gave up.

As she walked away, the unthinkable happened. A TVLand commercial announcing a *Little Guy Mike* weekend marathon was broadcast on the televisions throughout the bar.

"*Looking for 'Little Guy Mike'? Well we know where you can find him. Right here on TVLand!*"

Clay could not believe what he was seeing. His childhood face lit up the place.

"*It's a* Little Guy Mike *Weekend! 48 hours of back-to-back episodes!*"

The portly bartender got excited. "I love that show!"

Clay sunk into his bar stool trying to disappear.

College students began singing "One Dream Short — The Ballad of Little Guy Mike." Soon the whole bar joined in. Even Tommy knew the words!

"*One dream short from touching the sky. Then along came one lit-tle guy. And now the impossible is just around the bend. Thanks to our new lit-tle friend. He's our guy, aye, aye, lit-tle guy. He's our guy, aye, aye, lit-tle guy. Little Guy Mike!*"

Clay pulled down his knit hat, got up and quietly slipped out of the bar.

* * *

The street was crowded as he drove down University Avenue in Palo Alto. It was backed up from the weekly farmer's market. He moved slowly through the heavy traffic, the windows rolled down and the cold breeze blowing in his face.

Blasting the radio, he tried to get that damn theme song out of his head. It was insidious, designed to overtake any other thought. If anything made him want to run, it was that song. He spotted the Cal Trans train station in the distance.

The farmer's market was in full swing, bustling with families, seniors and the young professionals who lived and worked in the area. This had also become a weekly ritual for Becky, who took the train in after work and always headed to the flower vendor first. No matter what kind of day she was having, the sight of flowers was usually enough to lift her spirits. Besides, she liked carrying the flowers with her as she made her way through the rest of the market. This evening was no different.

It wasn't hard to spot the sunflowers beyond the Gerber daisies and peonies. She sorted through the buckets, her auburn hair tied in a scarf, waitress uniform peeking out from the oversized sweater she was wearing.

Finally, she held up two bunches of sunflowers, one in each hand. She shook off the excess water and took a moment to compare the two.

"The bunch on your left...."

Becky was surprised to discover Clay standing beside her, his confident eyes and defined jaw framed by the knit hat he was wearing.

"Clearly.... They're brighter, more confident...overall, a happier bunch." Clay offered a self-assured smile.

"And these...?" She held up the bunch in her right hand.

"They look *less* happy...kind of sad and insecure. They have fewer petals and leaves. Overall, I don't think they can give you what you need."

Becky studied both again and then, aware of her own need, made a confident choice: the *less* happy bunch in her right hand. "These," she told the vendor.

Clay was taken aback.

"They're lonely. They need me."

Clay had a sense that he had met his match. As the vendor tore a piece of brown butcher paper to wrap up the flowers, Clay subtly changed gears. "So I guess all I need to know is your address."

"I've had plenty of guys ask for my phone number, but my address?" Becky paid the vendor.

"Oh, I'm not asking you out. Did you think I was asking you out? I just need your address so I can deliver your 'lonely' flowers."

"Painful. You are so painful."

"Me? I looked like an idiot showing up with that coffee cake."

"I feel terrible." Becky bit her lip to contain her laughter.

"I'm sure you do."

Becky regained her composure. "So how's it going…at the church?"

"I'm in over my head. I think it's time to start planning my exit."

"That's too bad."

The vendor handed Becky the sunflowers.

"Look, while I am here, I really would like to see you again."

"I'm done dating guys who are just passing through. I've been there, done that."

"Don't think of it as passing through. Think of it as… drive-thru dating."

Becky gave him a stare before he could backtrack.

"Okay, maybe that's not a good analogy."

Becky shook her head. Somehow his goofiness was part of his charm.

"Come on."

But Becky wouldn't budge.

"All right…. All right. No dating," Clay made the official declaration. "There will be no dating!" After a moment, he tried another angle. "How about walking? Can I walk with you? No dating. Just walking?"

Becky was suspect, but somehow he had worn her down. "I guess that would be all right."

They made their way into the farmer's market.

"You know it's tough times for churches."

"Really…?"

"When I delivered the coffee cake, they didn't even tip."

Becky smiled.

* * *

A woman forged Clay's signature on to a box containing a *Little Guy Mike* action figure. She placed a "Certified Authenticated Signature" sticker on the back and then packed it in a carton for shipping.

She had told herself that she was going to go to bed early tonight, but she knew she still had a few hours of work ahead of her. Things always picked up whenever Clay was in the news. Although it had been years, any news was good news because at least it was news.

She gathered the rest of the packages for the post office that she would drop off in the morning. Settling at her computer, she uploaded snapshots of the new merchandise onto her website, CLAYHEART Auctions. The site had a reputation for selling both merchandise and rare personal items that once belonged to Clay.

The doorbell rang.

Getting up to answer the door, she passed family photos on the wall. The faded pictures were of a shy boy and his mother.

Patty Grant opened the door and was surprised to discover Burt standing before her. She tried to shut the door, but was blocked by Burt's foot in the doorjamb.

"I don't know where he is, and if I did, I wouldn't tell you," she snapped.

Burt glanced at all the packages in the entry. He cocked his head. "Some people would call you a terrible mom for how you make your living," he said sarcastically, "but not me. What else were you supposed to do when that kid took off and stopped supporting you?"

He inched his foot further in the door, feeling her ease her grasp.

"Leave him alone…"

"He owes me! He owes all of us!"

"I never should have trusted you," she whispered.

Burt pushed his way into the entry and pulled out his wallet.

"I don't need your money," Patty said without looking at him.

"He doesn't care about you! He doesn't care about anyone but himself!"

"That's not true…."

"When are you going to wake up? He made a fool out of all of us."

"It wasn't his fault."

Burt snapped his wallet shut and stuffed it in his jeans. "I *will* find him, with or without your help!" Burt took a good look at all the packages by the door before turning and walking way. "And when I do…"

Patty paused, and then called out to Burt with desperation in her voice, "Hey," Burt turned to look at her, anticipating a clue. "If you do find him…" She hesitated knowing that whatever she said could never make up for what she had done. Her voice faltered. "…never mind."

Patty watched as her only connection to her son turned and walked into the darkness. She closed the door.

* * *

Clay and Becky walked through the farmer's market passing arts and crafts, food and produce vendors. Although they were not on a date, it looked a lot like one.

A small crowd gathered around a jazz quartet playing Bossa Nova. The quartet was pretty good.

An older Jewish man with a thick Yiddish accent began humming along, his hands and head swaying to the unhurried rhythm. His spirit was contagious, transforming the high-brow mood into a joyful experience. He spotted Becky and began romancing her away from Clay.

Clay and Becky shared a smile before moving on.

They stopped at a gourmet tamale stand and split a blue corn tamale with green chili.

"Did you meet Max?" Becky asked.

"The guy in the ridiculous golfing clothes who looks like Randy Quaid?"

"He's my brother."

"Did I mention Randy Quaid is a good looking dude? Dennis Quaid has nothing on him. If you ask me Meg Ryan went for the wrong Quaid…"

"He's the only family I have. I moved here a few months ago after my dad passed."

"I'm sorry."

"I wasn't even living near my dad. I hadn't seen him in years. But once it happened…" Becky caught herself. "I don't even know why I'm telling you all this…"

"No, I appreciate it. Really."

"Once it happened, I felt like being closer to family." Becky glanced at her lonely sunflowers again. "Don't say anything, but he's thinking of moving."

"Would you go with him?"

Becky shook her head, no. "For once, I'm going to stay put. Besides, he has his own family, and I like it here."

"I don't want you to think I'm a quitter, but I'm in a tough situation." Maybe it was that she had opened up first, or perhaps he needed her to understand, but either way he felt he could trust her…at least with this. Without telling her the specifics, Clay explained his dilemma in the vaguest terms possible. "If I had known what they expected of me before I came, I probably never would have come."

"But you are here now?"

"It's not that easy."

Becky listened as they moved toward the candle vendor.

The tent was beautifully lit with the glimmering candles glowing against the night sky. They stopped and sniffed a few scents: pear, orange spice, jasmine.

"This assignment — it's hard to find the words."

"Look, it's none of my business, but have you tried? Really tried?"

"What would it change?"

Becky stared at the flickering candles. "When my dad was living, neither one of us could find the words. It's strange, now that he's gone, they come so easily. I catch myself talking to him all the time — only he's not there."

She glanced at Clay.

"It's important to find the words while they can still do some good."

* * *

"My homework?" Tyler spoke into the receiver. "It's coming along just fine, Mom."

Ted raised his head out of the elementary school textbook and shot Tyler a perplexed look. He sat at the dining room table beside the folded laundry and empty frozen dinner containers. A moment ago the answers were clear; now he was second-guessing himself.

"You know Dad's preaching this Sunday…and they're announcing it!"

Ted erased the answers he had just written, blowing the particles away.

"I already told you that?" Tyler said. He held his hand

over the phone and quietly pleaded with his dad. "Talk to her."

Ted looked up, staring at the receiver. Their last conversation hadn't gone well. Flight arrangements for the service quickly digressed into how she couldn't pretend everything was perfect anymore, that she didn't feel needed, that there was no place in his life for her, and how he always picked the church over her. He had told her that if she wasn't going to stay then she shouldn't come back for the funeral. He never thought she wouldn't be there.

Tyler held out the phone and waited. "Please…."

Ted reluctantly reached for the phone, but hesitated.

Tyler watched in disappointment as his dad abruptly got up from the table and left the room.

"Tyler, are you still there?" His mom's echo reverberated from the receiver.

"Yeah, Mom. I'm still here." The boy gripped the phone tighter. "I'm still here."

* * *

Clay walked Becky to the Cal Trans station. "Are you sure I can't give you a ride home?"

"It's only a few stops," she replied cradling her sunflowers.

"You don't know what you're passing up. Not everyone gets to ride in the High Hope truck."

Her hazel eyes lit up each time she smiled. It made him

want to do whatever he could to see that happen again.

They came near the platform passing a couple who gave them an "aren't you a romantic couple" smile.

"I know we're just 'walking and all,' but people could get the wrong idea," Clay said.

"How so…?" Becky didn't want to admit that she was feeling something stronger than she was letting on.

"Flowers…" he said quietly. He moved in closer.

She watched his eyes stare at her lonely bouquet.

"Moonlight…"

She followed his gaze upward, their eyes searching for the moon beneath the thick fog that was rolling in. They waited until they could spot its illuminated presence.

"An amazing woman…" Lowering his gaze, he looked at her, waiting for that brightness to re-appear in her eyes. When he saw it, he eased in for the kiss.

Becky hesitated, trying to remember her rationale for keeping emotional distance. "I don't kiss on the first…."

Clay placed his index finger gently on her lips. "This isn't a date, remember…."

Becky gripped her bouquet as he leaned in.

He kissed her softly. The vulnerability of the moment lingered before the embarrassment settled in.

The Cal Trans train approached the station.

"I better get going."

He watched her move towards the train.

"By the way, you were right," Clay said.

Becky looked back, gripping her bouquet.

"The sunflowers…. They look happier already." He saw

the brightness in her eyes as she boarded the train. As the platform emptied, Clay watched the train leave the station.

* * *

Heavy fog rolled in as Clay drove back to the church, the truck's headlights revealing only a few feet ahead of him as he traveled along the winding mountain road.

Parking the truck, he closed the old barn doors and walked across campus through the dense fog.

As he approached the memorial garden Diego had been busy working in, Clay thought he heard weeping.

Moving forward, he noticed that the whimsical iron gates were open. Through the thick fog he made out a figure. It was Ted. He was at his mother's grave, reading from a crumpled paper in his hand. It sounded like a eulogy.

"Everyone felt like she was their mother. But she was *my* mother." Ted took pride in the statement before continuing. "And she always saw — in all of us — what we could never see in ourselves. That was her gift."

Clay watched from a distance.

Ted looked lost as he stared at the memorial grave stone. Moving closer, he got down on bended knee.

Putting down the paper, Ted spoke to her as if she were there. It was a whole different Ted. "I'm sorry mom. I tried." He wept. "I'm always trying. But it doesn't matter. I can't make anything work." Ted was now sobbing. "I'm sorry. I'm just so sorry."

What had started out sounding like a eulogy had become a confession of sorts. Clay did not feel right listening in. He moved on in the dense cover of fog.

Clay returned to his loft apartment. Tossing the truck's keys on the dresser, he took out his wallet and removed a scrap of paper. Sitting on the side of the bed, he stared at the phone number. Picking up the receiver to the rotary phone, he began dialing. As the phone rang he felt a hesitation.

Two thousand miles away a woman turned on a lamp beside her bed and answered the phone. It was Patty Grant — his mother.

"Hello..."

Clay hesitated, the sound of her voice transporting him back to his youth.

"Hello...?" she repeated.

Clay hung up the phone.

Chapter Twenty-One

The Acorn was bustling with the usual morning rush, but he arrived when they first unlocked the doors, before the set-ups were on the tables and the coffee cake had come out of the oven.

It was empty except for his thoughts.

He settled into a booth, trying to separate himself not only from the patrons who would be trickling in, but from the sound of his mother's voice that had filled up his once-sacred loft.

Although it was a new day, it felt like a continuation from the night before. And the cellophane toothpicks overhead gave him no direction.

He knew better than to open any door to his past, and still he couldn't get beyond the image of Ted speaking to his mother through the thick fog. But Rose was a saint.

She hadn't exploited her own son and then abandoned him right when he needed her the most, turning him over to handlers with their own financial motives. He caught himself. He knew where that rabbit-hole led and wanted to bring as little of that junk into this new day as possible.

Turning his attention to the task at hand, he removed a pad of paper from his backpack and tried to see what he could come up with.

As the diner filled up, his table became covered with crumpled paper. Obviously, he was not having much luck. He found it hard to write while keeping those feelings at bay, the impossibility of opening up and shutting down at the same time. He knew he should be stronger, able to rise above it, but he just couldn't. And that is why he always tried to stay at least one step ahead of it.

Staring at a blank piece of paper, he got a thought and wrote it down.

"I always wanted to be a man of steel."

He stared at the page, trying to complete his thought… finally adding, "Unfortunately, I'm just Clay."

Crumpling up the paper, he added it to the pile.

Clay looked around the diner for inspiration. No luck.

He glanced at that art-deco mural above the counter, the rustic faces of city workers and ranch hands crossing paths in front of the feed store in the 1930's, painted golden rays shining down on both. He was always looking for a glimpse of Heaven, but had yet to find it.

Staring at their faces, it was as if they were trying to tell him something, that the promise hidden in their eyes was realized as they crossed paths in front of the feed store and that he belonged among them.

He admired the mural and its message of brotherhood, but thought about the paintings he had seen in the barn: the truth about the cruelty of man that was not exclusive to any race.

It occurred to him that he also could not write because he knew better than to be idealistic, understood the danger of believing in an idea divorced from the reality he always knew. For him, that only led to disappointment. The hope could never be sustained. In the end, people always hurt you. He concluded that the message of that mural — however beautiful — was imposed by the idealism of the artist. He didn't want to do the same.

A waitress approached him with a pot of coffee.

He quickly put his hand over his mug.

"Why stop now?" The waitress grimaced before moving on.

"I was afraid you'd start charging me for refills."

Turning his attention, he gazed out the window and spotted Becky crossing the street. Happily distracted, he watched her. He couldn't get over it. She was perfect: the hair, the hazel eyes, the legs, just the right combination of sweet and feisty that kept him on his toes. He didn't know if he was idealizing her or just really seeing who she was. He only knew that he was drawn to this quality in her that transcended everything else. It was hope dwelling in a place of sadness. To him, that meant more than anything else he had heard or seen.

She made her way into the diner, saying "hello" to her co-workers. Moving behind the counter, she placed her apron over her uniform and secured it.

Clay picked up his empty coffee cup, walked to the counter and took a seat. "What does a guy have to do to get a refill around here?"

Becky was surprised to see him.

"You didn't think I was going to skip town, not after last night?"

"I wasn't sure." She reached for the pot of coffee and filled his mug up. "I'm still not sure."

"This relationship is never going to work unless you have a little faith in me," he said half-jokingly.

Becky rolled her eyes. She thought he looked a little disheveled, like he hadn't slept, but somehow the look worked on him.

"I've been here all morning. I'm trying. I really am."

"Any luck…?" She noticed the pile of crumpled papers on his table.

Leaning over the counter, he whispered in her ear. "The words are in hiding. They don't want to be found. I don't blame them."

She looked at him with assurance. "Don't worry. You'll find them."

He perked up. "So you do have faith in me?"

Becky smirked.

"I'm thinking that the real problem isn't that I can't write it; it's that I have a problem getting people's hopes up." He glanced at the rustic faces in the mural again. "I want to be honest. I want to be true to my life experience. Unfortunately, that's not very inspirational." He caught himself. He couldn't believe he just admitted to a beautiful woman that he didn't think his life was very inspirational.

"But you said they want to hear your perspective?"

"Yeah, but this is going to be *public*, so I don't want to cause problems...."

"Maybe you don't need to worry about being inspirational. Maybe being honest is enough."

"The church is called 'High Hope,' not 'slightly disappointed.'"

The first waitress passed by and noticed Clay drinking another cup of coffee. She shook her head before moving on.

"I've had a few cups already," he admitted to Becky. It was an understated confession that fooled no one.

"I figured that," Becky said.

"Look, I have to work on this, but I thought maybe later tonight we could hang out again? Find another farmer's market or something—"

"I can't."

"You have plans?"

"It's not that. I told you last night. I can't pursue this any further...not if you're not going to be sticking around."

"Hey, this is a risk for me too. How do I know that once you really get to know me you won't dump me for the next lovable, slightly disappointed, scruffy-faced hunk that comes to town?"

"I guess the only way you'll know for sure is if you stick around."

He rolled his eyes. "I don't like it, but I'll respect it. I won't try to change your mind…. I promise." Clay smirked.

* * *

Alexis, Max, Thomas, Maggie, Paul and Monica exited the day's staff meeting that had just ended, pausing in the corridor as Reagan, Ted and the rest of the staff continued on. They shared glances, somehow surprised that Reagan had not come to his senses.

"Maybe Reagan's setting Ted up?" Thomas was always the conspiracy theorist.

Alexis shook her head no.

"Think about it. Get him up to bat quick. Strike him out fast. It makes sense."

"At least it makes some sense," Max said.

Maggie was insistent. "No father is going to sacrifice his son…even if it is for the sake of the church."

Max glanced at her. "We really need to rent you *The Passion of The Christ*."

Maggie looked confused as the group laughed.

"So Max…" Monica changed the subject, "word has it that Pearl Street Pond's come a calling."

Max looked at Alexis.

"I swear it wasn't me," Alexis said.

"That's not something I want made public right now," Max said. "Especially in light of everything that's going on here."

"Hey, we all did our best," Paul said. "If this place implodes, our hands are clean."

Alexis glared at him. "I just watched you eat a hunk of coffee cake without a fork."

Paul took stock of his buttery hands. "Well, you get my point."

"So why wasn't Mr. Ironside in staff meeting?" Thomas inquired.

"Reagan has him on 'special assignment,'" Alexis informed the group.

* * *

Clay held the ladder in front of the Acorn steady, staring at her shapely legs. He knew he should be writing, but this was a welcome distraction.

As Becky hammered above, he hummed, doing his best impression of the Yiddish man from the night before.

"*Ya, da, da, da, ya, da, da, ya, ya…*"

"Stop humming that."

"*Not until you go out with me,*" his request interspersed with humming.

"That guy was charming. You're like one of those annoying boys I used to beat up on the playground."

Becky held out her hand.

"I'm trying. That has to count for something." Clay handed her the flag pole.

"I've lost a lot of people in my life. Honestly, I can't take it."

"Well, what am I supposed to do until I do know if I'm staying put?" He helped her down the ladder.

Becky thought for a moment, conjuring up a suitable compromise. "You can always visit me at the counter."

"The counter?" Clay balked with lovable outrage.

"The counter is a great place to hang out."

She stepped off the ladder and took a look at the patchwork flag. It read: Welcome.

He glanced at the flag and then back at Becky, but was feeling anything but welcome. "What is so *special* about the counter?"

"Do you know what I see when I work the counter?"

"People chewing?"

Becky moved towards the plate glass window. "Most of the time I see an amazing mix of people."

Clay followed. He stared at the counter through the window. It was full. He could see people's backs and side profiles.

"Every kind of person you can imagine — all lined up, seated side by side."

He noticed the eclectic mix of people, eating breakfast, engaged in conversation. He saw an elderly man sharing a word with an Indian woman who smiled before repeating what he said to a business man next to her.

"People who would never interact outside of this place, taking time to come together, share a bit of their lives…a bit of their lives with some stranger on the left or right of them. To me, that's holy."

"I don't think I'm ever going to look at a diner the same way again."

"Don't get me wrong, this job can be a drag. But there are those moments."

"That's beautiful. Can I steal it?"

Becky held up the hammer. "Those are my words. You have to find your own."

"The problem with my words is that they sound too much like me. I can't do this. I was sitting at that counter, and I didn't see any of that. In fact, I was annoyed at how close everyone was to me."

"Well, I guess that's my answer." Becky took a seat on the bench.

"Don't give up on me yet."

* * *

Ted proudly held his sermon in hand as he walked down the corridor towards his father's office.

He passed Monica.

"Looking forward to Sunday, Ted!" Monica said offering an enthusiastic 'thumbs-up' as she passed.

"Why thank you, Monica." Ted was flattered. The announcement had gone out, so he knew people in town would be talking by now. Maybe he had more support than he had imagined.

Reagan was on the phone when Ted knocked on his open door. Reagan had spent the day putting out fires and the largest one had yet to ignite.

"You wanted to see me?" Ted said.

Reagan stared at his son with a pensive look. "Have a seat...."

"I almost have my talk committed to memory, but of course I want it loaded in the teleprompter just in case."

"About that message...I think we should save it for another day."

"Another day...?" Ted knew he should have seen this coming. With his father there was always a catch. "Let me guess, I'm not preaching anymore...."

"Indeed, you are...just not that." Reagan pointed to his sermon. "I want to set you up to win. That's the other Ted... not the real Ted that we want to introduce to everyone."

Gripping the sermon, Ted knew it would be scrapped just like the eulogy he had composed for his mother.

"I expect you to trust me on this," Reagan said.

Ted's eyes widened. "But if I'm not writing it...who is?"

* * *

The sign out front announced the mid-day mass. Clay crossed the street and made his way into the modest Catholic Church in downtown Cliff Falls.

Mass was in progress. The sparse parish stood reciting a prayer. These were the faithful. They were at church in the middle of the day, and it wasn't even a holiday. He moved down the side aisle as light poured in through the stained glass windows.

Trying to be discreet, he slipped into a pew beside an elderly woman with very clear diction. He tried to follow along, but the prayer was slightly different than the one he was familiar with. The elderly woman gave him an encouraging smile as he stumbled through it.

For all his criticism of High Hope, it did occur to him that this place could use a television or two so visitors could follow the prayer. And while they were at it, better lighting and a new sound system. But he didn't want to be a critic. It was just that they obviously had the "holy" down and he thought they could benefit from some better production values. But again, he didn't want to be critical. Just when he was done re-imagining the mass as a state-of-the-art production event, the parish took their seats.

"He who began a good work in you will carry it out until completion."

Father Sam started his homily from the vestibule. He was thin and looked tired. If not for the clerical collar, he would blend into any crowd. There was nothing remarkable about the silver-haired man, except the subtle Creole accent that seemed misplaced coming out of an otherwise Irish man.

"In our first reading, Paul reminds us that we are mere vessels for God's great purpose and that our confidence and trust must remain not in ourselves, but in Him."

He noticed that the more passionate the man became,

the stronger his Creole accent revealed itself. Clay was confident that he spent years working with the poor in New Orleans. For him, this hidden history from an otherwise unremarkable man was all the credibility he needed.

Reaching for an offering envelope and miniature pencil, he began scribbling away. He had learned a trade secret from all those years on set: namely, how writers and producers recycled storylines from other popular shows. In fact, the writers were always reading through other scripts, finding ways to tweak a concept just enough to fit the show and not result in legal action. By the end of the run, the writers were actually tweaking storylines they had already done in earlier seasons. He hated the practice, engaging in legendary arguments that halted production, but had recently grown to appreciate its merits.

"We must get out of the way, and let God work in and through us."

Clay wrote as fast as he could, his fingers cramping from the miniature pencil. Soon the offering envelope was covered with his plagiarized notes. He found his answer. He wasn't going to disappoint anyone, not Reagan, not Becky and especially not Tyler. Whatever the outcome, they would have at least known that he tried, even if "technically" he was "re-purposing" another guy's message. But that was beside the point. This was for the greater good, so he was willing to bet God wouldn't nail him on a technicality. For once he was a happy man.

"Finally, let me make this clear." The Creole accent was undeniably evident as the Irish priest made his last point with authority.

Clay mouthed Father Sam's words as he wrote, quietly mimicking his Creole accent. "Finally, let me make this clear."

"There are *no short cuts* in this work God has called you to do."

"There are *no short cuts*...." Clay looked up from scribbling as the words slowly sunk in.

"It is a charge that no one can do for you. You must do it for yourself!"

If not for the authority in his voice, Clay might have ignored the warning, but this old priest had gotten the better of him.

Conviction washed over Clay's face.

Reaching into his pocket, he pulled out a crumpled five dollar bill. He stuffed it into his note-covered envelope and sealed it — along with his fate — tossing it into the offering basket as the usher approached.

The elderly woman beside him noticed what he had done. She whispered in bewilderment, "But you took such good notes."

He watched as his last best hope made its way down the aisle in a wire basket.

Chapter Twenty-Two

The mass ended, although a few parishioners slipped out after taking communion. Clay remained in the pew, devastated. He was out of options, and he knew it. He didn't know what to do. Should he run or tell them he couldn't do it?

Confiding in the elderly woman who stayed behind, he explained his dilemma in the vaguest terms possible. The woman was a good listener.

"I can't use his words, and I can't find my own. This is going to get ugly. It always does."

The woman's kind but stern face was a subtle reminder to him of Rose.

"*Nothing gold stays…*" Clay said. "That's from *The Outsiders.*"

The former school teacher corrected him. "I think it was Robert Frost."

"Him too?"

All he felt was the disappointment of everyone he would be letting down. It was a familiar feeling that always overwhelmed him. As much as he tried, he couldn't get Tyler's disappointed face out of his mind; the same must have been on Bella's face every time she remembered his broken promise to her.

"You should go to confession."

Clay was defensive at the suggestion. "This is *not* my fault this time—"

"It cleans out the pipes…"

"—I don't need confession. Words…I need words."

The woman took a dollar bill out from her purse. Standing up, she patted him on the shoulder. "I'll light you a candle."

He glanced at the illuminated votives in the distance: red and gold glass on one side and blue and white on the other. They were the glimmering prayers of hope.

There was only one other thing he could do, but he was unsure if he had it in him, unsure if it would work. He knew it was what Reagan was betting on all along. Rose must have told him. But they didn't know how much he had changed in those years, how callous a bruised spirit can become when everything that was unacknowledged remains swept under the rug. Besides, he didn't know if he was willing to go there, or what he'd find if he did…or worse yet, if he'd be able to get back.

He watched as the woman made her way down the side aisle and lit the candle, the flickering flame melting the hardened wax.

* * *

"He can't write something like this." Ted pleaded with his father. It was like Reagan had brought Clay to Cliff Falls just to make a fool out of Ted. "How do you even know he has a relationship with God?"

"I'm betting that if he doesn't, he will by the time he writes the message," Reagan said.

"Your belief in him is overwhelming." Ted had fought his whole life for such confidence from his father. The moment he thought he had it, he realized it had slipped through his fingers. "The church is going to know I didn't write it. Have you considered the damage when people find out?"

"I'm prepared for the fallout should that occur."

Ted picked up a Bible from his father's desk and waved it. "What translation are you reading because I don't recall a former-child-star protection program in here?"

"Careful how you wave that book, Theodore. It's supposed to be Good News."

"You're hiding him. How do you justify that?"

"The woman caught in adultery: Jesus didn't humiliate her. He protected her. God doesn't expose people....He covers them. Ted, you know this."

Ted glanced at the Bible in his hand.

"I know that isn't the church I built, but it is what we must become."

"And we're starting with Clay?" Ted said.

"What is it that you object to? That he may not be able to write it, or that I'm giving the boy a chance?"

Ted struggled to look past his own resentment.

"He is more like you than you know," Reagan said. "That boy carried the weight of the world on his shoulders. And the people who handled him, well, they were not kind. Ted, you do remember, don't you?"

All Ted remembered was that *one* afternoon. He hadn't given it much thought in years.

Reagan and Rose were already at the stadium. Ted had stayed behind. He sat on the hotel bed working on his college applications, self-conscious of the bright abstinence t-shirt he was wearing that read: "I'm not doin' it!"

He was reviewing the corrections his father had made to his essay when he heard yelling in the hallway. "You little shit! You've done it now!"

Fixing his eyes on the page, he tried to concentrate but the voice grew louder.

"You're dead! When I get my hands on you…!"

Ted was startled when the adjoining door burst open.

Clay sprang into the room, quickly shutting the door as he caught his breath. He glanced at Ted across the room. "Nice t-shirt."

"What do you think you're doing?"

"I'm just passing through…." Clay moved to the front door, opened it briefly, and then promptly shut it. "Correction, I'm hiding…"

"There is a stadium of kids waiting to see you. They're going to sing happy birthday and everything."

"It's a bitch being a kid. The sooner they find that out the better."

The voice in the hallway grew louder. "You little shit! I swear, when I find you—"

Clay desperately searched for a place to hide. After a moment, he crawled under the bed Ted was sitting on.

"You can't—" Ted objected, wanting no part in this mess.

"Preacher kid, help a guy out…."

"My name is Ted."

Clay stuck his head out from under the bed, his eyes revealing the seriousness of the situation. "Ted…. Cover for me. Please, hide me."

Ted saw the fear in his eyes.

The adjoining door burst open, just as Clay slid back under the bed, his terrified eyes betraying the darkness of the hidden space.

Maybe the signs were there that summer. Maybe for some events only the passing of time revealed their significance.

* * *

The golden rays poured in through the stained glass windows warming the side of Clay's face, but he barely noticed.

The church was empty. He sat there in the wooden pew, staring blankly in the distance as the words seeped in. He felt safe in the stillness, safe enough to listen.

When he was younger he used to wait for the words to

come. He would return to the backlot after dark, finding refuge atop the rusty scaffolding behind the façade-lined streets. He would write into the early morning hours, in a time when God still spoke to him and the words came easily. But as time passed, he was never still long enough for the words to arrive.

Now in the sacred silence he waited like he had done when he was a boy, with an open mind, heart and spirit. But the only words that came to him were the ones given the night of the fire.

> *...scared children — all of us — dealing with adult things — wondering if we are that strong. And everyone wants us to be someone or something else....*

Those words had returned to him numerous times in the years that followed, but he always resisted letting them in. They were a link to his past and an unfortunate truth that he knew he could do nothing about. They made him feel helpless, and he hated that.

Here he was now, opening himself up, desperately waiting for a new word, but the same phrase repeated in his spirit, each time accompanied by a flood of memories that threatened to overwhelm him.

> *...scared children — all of us — dealing with adult things — wondering if we are that strong. And everyone wants us to be someone or something else....*

He was no longer alone in the church, the accusing faces and voices from his youth filling the pews around him. He had known better than to open this door to the past. It felt cruel, as if he had been given a stone when he had asked for a loaf of bread.

Staring at the illuminated candles located throughout the church, he was curious if all prayers were answered in this way, or maybe just his prayers?

He didn't exactly blame God for not speaking to him anymore. He just didn't understand what he was supposed to do, what God expected from him.

All Clay knew was what he didn't want, and at the top of that list was not feeling this junk again. *What was the purpose?* If not for a few scars on his back or the way he instinctively cowered when he heard a sudden noise, he may have convinced himself that nothing ever happened. Or worse yet, whatever did occur he had brought upon himself.

It was amazing how incredibly confusing everything could get, how uncertain the certain could become.

Maybe they were right? Maybe they were all right?

His angry eyes rose above the flickering flames that surrounded him. He realized that along the walls, to the right and left of him, were ceramic interpretations of the paintings he discovered in the barn, each unjust moment memorialized in Spanish glazed tile. He had been sitting in the midst of them the whole time and hadn't even noticed.

Clay wondered who had commissioned the hidden paintings displayed in the hallways of his own mind. He hated to admit it, but that stuff was always with him and always around him.

He thought about running, but where would he go?

He had been willing to open up, wait for the words to come, but these memories were all he got. He tried to tell himself that he didn't care, that this wasn't his problem and that he had been brought here under false pretenses, but the feelings wouldn't dissipate. He just kept picturing Tyler's face.

He stared at the gilded crucifix above the altar; it was hope taking its last breath.

After a few moments, he noticed Father Sam walk down the aisle and go into the confessional. From the pew, he watched the green light turn on.

Clay opened the carved wooden door, but hesitated, surprised by the setup. It didn't look like it did in the movies. The intimate room resembled a counseling office with two chairs facing each other. This was one modern improvement he could have done without.

He couldn't believe he was doing this but was willing to go through with it in the hope that God might relent and allow him to find the words for that kid's sake. Besides, how hard could this be? Fess up, get yelled at, and get out.

He noticed that Father Sam was not making eye contact, so he crossed the threshold and eased into the seat. He was intrigued by the man and thought about talking to him, but, now inside, felt the gravity of what this was all about.

"In the name of the Father, Son and Holy Spirit…"

Clay had played a dyslexic Irish orphan named "Scully" on a Network Afternoon Special called "Not Without My Sling Shot" with George Hamilton as the neighborhood priest. Admittedly, it was a stretch for both of them. But in this moment he would have done anything to confess "Scully's" sins instead. Maybe he could excuse himself, buy a slingshot, break a window and come back? One thing was certain, honesty was easier when he was playing a character and the priest chastising him was a man with a tan. But this was the real thing, and Father Sam was obviously not a sun dweller.

Lowering his head, he searched his heart, trying to discern his own thoughts from the accusing voices that had filled the church on the other side of the door. He closed his eyes to concentrate, but could only see the hidden paintings from his youth: the collection of moments that lead up to the night of the fire….

Father Sam waited in the silence, but heard nothing. "Have you done something?"

"Well, when I was a teenager I did start a fire that burned down part of a Hollywood studio backlot."

The Irish priest couldn't help but look up.

"It was an accident, and, trust me, I've been paying for it ever since."

Father Sam lowered his gaze again.

Clay sorted through his sins as if he were searching for the ugliest one beneath it all. He knew what God saw when He looked at him. It was endless: the tantrums, the women, the self-centered choices that he had become famous for. The remorse was real, but it didn't bring relief.

"There are plenty of things I'm not proud of, but it's more than that." He tried to put his finger on it, but he just couldn't. "I'm just sorry. I'm just always sorry."

The Irish priest pressed him again. "Sorry for what?"

He looked up in frustration. "I'm sorry I'm me."

Father Sam glanced up.

Even Clay was surprised by what he had blurted out. "I am. I think I always have been. I don't know how else to explain it."

Clay felt a strange mix of relief and anxiety. Suddenly his question had become so clear. "I don't know how this thing works, but can you do that?"

Father Sam recognized the desperation in his eyes.

"Can you absolve me for being me?"

"You want me to absolve you for being you?" The silver-haired man gazed at him in disbelief.

"You think if you could just change the things you do, the things you've done, that it will make the difference. It never does. It's hard, holding yourself together, when so many of those pieces are…*flawed.* And you start to turn on yourself in so many little ways. You get really tired of disappointing people."

The priest lowered his head, but Clay interrupted him.

"One more thing…I'm not Catholic."

"You're not Catholic?" The priest stared at him in confusion.

"There is this kid I made a promise to, and I just thought that if I did this, God might relent and let me not disappoint him. Besides, I needed my pipes cleaned. And I trust you."

"You may not be Catholic, but I am still going to give you penance. You do know what penance is, right?" Father Sam's voice was surprisingly stern.

Clay nodded yes, convinced he'd been paying it most of his life.

"You are to spend the remainder of this day envisioning God Himself repeating these words to you: 'You are my beloved son, in whom I am well pleased.'"

Father Sam's voice echoed in Clay's mind, challenging the chorus of voices flowing up from his past. The hidden paintings from Clay's youth emerged at the forefront of his mind. The phrase was challenging every other voice he had been convinced was true.

Clay hesitated as the words seeped in.

"You are my beloved son, in whom I am well pleased."

Through the rain soaked window, Clay watched his mother get on the bus.

He raised his head, looking directly at Father Sam.

"You are my beloved son, in whom I am well pleased."

Clay walked off set. A callous hand grabbed him, throwing him up against the wall. The terror was visible in his eyes.

Clay started to tear up, a part of him wanting to believe, another wanting the priest to shut up.

"You are my beloved son, in whom I am well pleased."

Clay's youthful face basked in the orange glow of the blaze, staring blankly into the fire. He watched as the plastic Halloween mask slowly melted.

Sobbing, Clay realized that the mask was gone that night, but what was underneath still needed to be healed.

"It's true. You can believe it." Father Sam leaned forward. "Sometimes it's too much. Our emotions, our minds, our bodies…they just can't take it. God knows His children get scared. Sin *is* sin, but it's okay to be human. You don't have to apologize for that."

Tears continued to drip from Clay's eyes.

"It can be hard to believe we'll ever get well, especially when we see our wounds for what they really are."

Father Sam pulled from under his chair a box of Kleenex and handed it to Clay.

"This is hard stuff. But you're getting honest, and He's meeting you where you are right now, dusting off the sin and everything that has made us *less* human. And once more we begin to believe, we see Him, and we see ourselves for who we really are: beloved children of God. Go in peace."

* * *

Clay squinted from the bright sun as he exited the church, somehow embarrassed that he gotten so emotional.

The priest had been very kind, but was he really going to spend the rest of the afternoon repeating that phrase in his head? He found that in spite of himself, he did just that.

He felt ridiculous, walking around town, telling himself that he was beloved, but he did it anyhow.

He said it as he passed the Cliff Falls Library and again when he reached the town square.

He said it as he sat on a bench in the park, watching the children play on the playground.

"You are my beloved son, in whom I am well pleased."

He said it again and again and again.

And each time he did, the vivid memories and accusing voices returned, but he just kept repeating it, allowing the words to enter his spirit and permeate him in an unexpected way.

Soon he wasn't repeating it anymore, he was hearing it. And it wasn't his own voice, it was another; one more tender.

"You are my beloved son, in whom I am well pleased."

As people passed him on the street, he pictured God saying it to them. "You are my beloved daughter. You are my beloved son."

The voice was so strong, he wondered if they could hear it.

He stopped by the Acorn, but didn't go inside. He just glanced at the counter and faces in the mural overhead.

"You are my beloved son, in whom I am well pleased."

"Scared children — all of us — dealing with adult things — wondering if we are that strong. And everyone wants us to be someone or something else, but...you are my beloved son, in whom I am well pleased." He shook his head. It was the rest of the phrase.

Clay made his way up the rustic trail, the words repeating in his spirit. He noticed the magnificent oaks that lined his path. In the stillness, he listened to the quiet rustling of leaves as he continued along the trail. Soon he came upon the rushing falls the city was named for. Three separate falls emanating from one source. The sight was majestic.

Light filtered through the golden oak leaves above the rushing waters. Standing on a rock, he could see his shadow on the opposite bank of the river. The roar of the water plunging over the cliff; the outflow emptying into the river, cascading over the falls... Everything he was carrying was being swept away. The mighty roar was consuming him. The mighty roar was calling out his name.

"You are my beloved son, in whom I am well pleased."

The falls made everything come alive. He breathed in deeply. It was as if he was taking his first breath.

* * *

By the time he had made his way back into town, something had changed. He had changed.

The falls were flowing through him now. It was like he had sunk deep beneath the water, gasping for air, but had come up the other side. It wasn't safe, it wasn't supposed to be. But it would be all right, and he wouldn't be alone.

He didn't know which had been more frightening: God or life?

When he was underneath he was alone, and it was scary and for a few moments, unbearable. But then he emerged, and he was all right and somehow changed. The transformation that had eluded him, like all observers who stand on the banks, was finally there. Knowing who you are not, Clay realized, was always the beginning of change; but until you hear your true name, you will wander, and perhaps, all should for a time.

* * *

Clay sat at the counter at the Acorn, thinking. After a few moments, he leaned over to a woman working at a nearby table and borrowed a pen. She was out of paper, so he started writing on a napkin.

He spent the afternoon writing.

Returning to his church campus apartment, he turned the light on and then placed a borrowed laptop labeled "Property of Max. Do not remove!" on his desk.

After turning it on, he began removing scraps of paper from his pocket, the sum of which comprised his message.

Clay was deep in thought. He passionately transferred his message into the laptop from the scraps of paper that lined his desk. After a moment, he stopped to relish in the quiet pride of something he wrote. He had found the words that resonated and the place from which they flowed.

* * *

Lots were cast worldwide as the bidding wars raged on.

"A 'Little Guy Mike' Halloween mask"
$232   1d   8h   10m
"A TV Guide featuring Clay on the cover"
$165   2d   3h   4m
"LGM Jacket worn by Clay"
$200   5d   13h   22m
"*Little Guy Mike* Microphone"
$23   6d   2h   14m

Ted stared at the computer screen in his office, unable to understand why the world still cared so much about Clay Grant. Nor could he understand why Clay fought so hard against it.

He sat there feeling sorry that he didn't recognize the signs of abuse all those years ago; but he was a kid with his own problems. Why should his reputation be at risk just so his father could assuage his guilt?

Ted stared out his office window. What did his father see in him? Reagan was always too busy for Ted. For as hard as Ted always tried to gain his father's support, Clay had it effortlessly. Maybe he did envy him, but the guy had everything and now he even had his father.

* * *

A solitary figure strolled across the vast church campus lawn. Clay stopped at Ted's office noticing that the light was on. He slipped the message under the door. Walking away, he couldn't help but feel good about what he had accomplished.

* * *

Clay was already in bed when he heard the first knock at his door. It was amazing how fast a new-found peace could be disturbed. He thought about ignoring it, but it persisted. Turning on the lamp, he got up and opened it.

Ted was seething. He gripped the message in his hand. "What gives you the right?"

Clay didn't follow. Ted's anger seemed out of proportion for what Clay tried to convey. "I just tried to write something that was honest. People can't relate to an image of perfection. Trust me I know."

"I've given this church everything; my childhood, my parents, my life. I'm not giving them this."

"What are you talking about?"

"I'd go to my father, but I know he'd just back you up." There was desperation in his eyes. "So I'm appealing to you, hoping something inside your selfish being will do the right thing."

"The right thing…?"

"I'll get you whatever cash you need. I don't care if I have to mortgage my house. But I want you gone by morning."

"What did I do wrong?"

"As far as we are concerned, you never wrote this."

"And if I don't leave?"

"Don't force my hand."

The threat didn't go unnoticed. Normally, Clay would have been out the door, but something inside of him had changed. He was proud of what he had written and was not going to be run off so easily.

"If you've been dealt such a raw deal, why don't you leave?" Clay said.

"Because some people live with the choices they make, even if they can't remember when or where they made them. They can't afford to be reckless because people depend upon them. But what would you know about that? By the time the impact hits, you're a hundred miles away."

"I'm done living like that. I know who I am now, and I don't care what you or anyone else has to say about it."

"This isn't just about you! You have no idea what's at stake here."

"Don't tell me you believe what Tyler does?" Clay said with sarcasm.

"What's that?"

"That if you do a really good job, your wife is going to come back."

"I pray everyday, that she never comes back."

It was a stunning admission. Clay stared at Ted in confusion.

"Because I know if she does, it will only be to take Tyler with her. He's all I have. This lousy church is all I have." He waved the message in his hand. "If I look like a fool, I will lose everything."

"You really expect me to leave?"

"What's the difference? At some point you're just going to run anyhow. That's what you do. That's what you've always done, isn't it?"

Clay stood there silent.

"For once in your life, do something selfless. Go now." Ted clenched the message in his hand. "I'm begging you. Leave this place."

Chapter Twenty-Three

Becky wrote the daily specials on the chalk board, playfully decorating the perimeter with happy, yellow chalk sunflowers.

"He bakes…?" one of Becky's co-workers said.

"He used to work in an Italian bakery. We already have our first official date planned out — should that occur. He's going to teach me how to make authentic pastries: tiramisu, biscotti…"

"What's wrong with our tiramisu?" She pointed to the California-version in the pastry case.

"Clay says that you never know you've got the fake thing, unless you've had the real thing."

"Sounds like a cola commercial."

"That's what I said. Apparently, one bite of an authentic Italian pastry and I won't be able to look at that other stuff again. The real thing is supposed to change my life."

"Sounds like it already has...."

Amid the crowd, a man sat at the counter eating a sandwich.

The waitress approached him. "Will that be all?"

Burt looked up as he chewed the last of his sandwich.

* * *

Clay was almost packed. Placing the last of his clothes in his duffel bag, he zipped it. He couldn't get past it. He had done everything they asked him to do, and he was still being sent away.

He stayed up half the night deciding whether to stay for Reagan or leave for Ted, but as the sun emerged over the hillside his choice became clear. Why was it that for Clay the selfless thing to do was to disappear?

Putting on his backpack, he took one last look around, the twin bed and night stand, and the bare desk beneath the vast window where he composed his message. He was going to miss this place. Glancing at the old television set with aluminum covered rabbit ears, he smirked.

He had written Reagan a letter, but decided not to leave it. He didn't want to cause any more problems, so he just slipped it in his backpack. It was better for everyone if they just assumed that he ran, better for everyone that was, except for Clay.

Moving to the window, he looked out over the

mountainous landscape, staring at that bubbling creek before turning to leave.

* * *

Reagan was coming up the steps to Clay's apartment, hoping to get a preview of what he had composed. It wasn't that he doubted him; he just wanted to look it over before Ted. Besides, he thought he could help smooth out any rough spots or Biblical inconsistencies. He went to knock on the door, but realized that it was open. Stepping inside, he found it empty. There was not a trace of Clay anywhere.

Reagan blamed himself. Obviously he had expected too much of the boy, thinking he could write it, and that drove him off. What had he done? Everything he had set in motion would unravel. If ever Reagan needed Rose it was now.

As he turned to leave, he noticed the trash pail beside the bare desk. It was filled with scraps of paper, each one covered in hand-written scribbling. Crouching down, Reagan read through the scraps.

* * *

Diego and a crew were busy working among the thorny shrubs in the memorial garden installing the last section of the whimsical iron gate along the perimeter. It was hot and the work was very physical.

He was sweating and catching his breath when he noticed a man taking pictures of the property. As the crew took a break, Diego walked over to the man.

"Afternoon…" Diego said wiping the sweat from his brow. "They sell postcards in the gift shop."

Burt lowered his camera. He was cautious not to ask just anyone. He didn't want to tip Clay off. "This is such a beautiful church. It would be a shame if something happened to it."

Diego looked at him bewildered.

"Do you watch much television?"

* * *

Ted glanced at the message on the desk, trying to justify what he had done the night before. He hadn't expected for it to affect him so deeply. It had become too personal to him. It was like Clay was in his head.

He wondered if Clay had actually left, but then he heard his father and Tyler in the corridor. His heart began to race.

"He's gone, Dad. He's gone."

Reagan didn't have to ask. Ted's guilt-ridden face gave him away.

"I know," Ted said quietly.

Tyler stared at his father in bewilderment. "Why would he leave? He promised."

Reagan held his tongue.

"I'll explain everything to you later. Right now, I need

to talk to your grandfather."

"He didn't even say goodbye," Tyler said.

"He had to leave in a hurry," Ted replied.

"Everyone around here leaves in a hurry." Tyler left disappointed.

Reagan waited for the boy to leave. "I won't stand for you running him off. What did you say to him?"

Ted picked up the message on the desk. "Did you read this?"

Reagan looked away.

"You'll go to any length to make sure Clay isn't exploited, but me—"

"You don't understand."

"Just say it. You have no confidence in me."

"That's not true."

"No, it is true. My words...my voice...they have never been enough. I've never been enough."

"You can't see it now, but I am doing this for you. I am for you, not against you. Son, I need you to believe that."

Ted was not convinced.

"Sending Clay off...I know this is not the man you want to be. This is not the example you want to set for Tyler." Reagan knew they were wasting time. "You can change this. Be the better man."

Ted stared blankly out the window, his father's reflection visible in the glass. "That's the problem. I've never been the better man."

"You were that night." Reagan leaned in. "When your mother passed—I looked for any excuse to leave. Ted, she was my strength, and the moment she was gone, my strength was gone. I couldn't face you or anyone else. So I left. But not you…you stayed."

"Why him…?"

"Helping Clay, it wasn't my idea. It was your mother's."

Reagan stared at his son's reflection in the glass. "You are so much like her. I just wanted everyone to see that."

* * *

Diego held the blurry photograph in his hand, staring at the green eyes.

"I'm telling you, he's trouble. I know. He destroys everything in his path."

Burt handed him others, pictures of Clay disguised in sunglasses, a knit hat, and of course the last one, covered in flour.

"What makes you think he'd be here?"

"He loves the mountains, the open space. Probably from all those years cooped up in a studio. Besides, I have a reliable tip."

Diego handed Burt back his pictures.

"Someone is helping him. If he's not in Cliff Falls now, he was." Burt pulled his wallet out and removed three one-hundred dollar bills. "You're sure you haven't seen him?"

Diego refused the money. "I haven't seen the man you describe. I can tell you that for certain."

"If he does show up, I hope you have good fire insurance," Burt said.

Burt handed Diego his card. "Call me if you hear anything, and I'll make it worth your trouble."

Burt took a few more photographs before making his way back down the hill.

* * *

The bell on the door jingled as Clay stepped into the diner. Once again he was carrying his duffle bag and backpack. It was against his better judgment, but he knew he couldn't leave without saying goodbye. He owed it to her, but he just didn't know if he could go through with it. He gripped his duffel bag as the door slowly shut. This was the point of no return.

Becky was working the counter. She had just finished taking an order when she looked up and noticed him. It took her a moment, but she had seen this scene before.

Clay stood there speechless.

"Let me guess, tiramisu and a phonebook?" Becky caught herself. "What am I thinking? Scratch the tiramisu; just the phonebook."

He couldn't even look at her.

She retrieved the yellow pages from under the counter and dropped it on the table next to him.

He couldn't help but glance at the glossy picture of the rushing falls on the cover, for a moment forgetting he had stumbled upon the real falls the day before and the change that he was certain was lasting. The disappointment was overwhelming. He looked at her speechless knowing that his best of intentions were never good enough, especially when he was the problem.

Becky waited for him to say something…anything. But there was just silence. "That's all right," she said quietly, "I know how hard it is for you to find the words."

She turned to walk away, angry at herself for not knowing better, for allowing herself to get that close to him.

"Becky…"

She hesitated, hoping for words other than what was spoken.

"I'm sorry."

Becky turned to the other waitress. "Cover for me."

The waitress nodded.

Becky held back tears as she walked out of the diner.

He didn't run after her. He just stood there frozen. It was better for her to hate him. He couldn't show it, but this was killing him. He watched as she left the diner.

Reaching into his pocket, he pulled out a dollar and turned to the waitress. "Can I get some change? I need to call a cab."

She looked at him with contempt.

"Never mind."

Parking his car along Ridge Road, Ted was wondering where to begin looking when he spotted Clay through the plate glass window of the Acorn

Diner. He took a deep breath before stepping inside.

Clay felt the anger well up inside of him when he noticed Ted in the doorway.

"Look, I owe you an apology," Ted said approaching him.

"I can't do this."

"I'm apologizing here…"

"It doesn't matter now. You're too late," Clay said, thinking of Becky. "Besides, you were right. This was a mistake."

Clay turned to leave, but remembered the letter he had written Reagan in his backpack. He hadn't planned to leave it, but now that Ted was here, it would give him closure. Slipping off his backpack, he unzipped it and retrieved the letter. "Do me a favor. Give this to your father and tell him thank you."

Ted took the folded letter.

"In fact, thank the whole staff for me." He paused, smiling. "Especially Diego. He's a good man."

Clay reached for this duffel bag. "And Tyler…just tell him he was right…a church isn't a very good hiding place."

Clay took one last look around, glancing at the watchful faces in the mural overhead. He had just started to believe there might be a place for him at the counter.

Turning to leave, Clay knew he had to tell Ted the truth. "For the record, that message wasn't about you. It was about me."

Ted stood there overwhelmed, holding the folded letter in hand as Clay walked out of the diner. Even if he really wanted to, Ted didn't know how to make him stay. He never knew how to make people stay.

Ted wavered, but he needed to know what Clay had written to his father. Unfolding it, he settled into a booth and quickly became engrossed.

"Until you showed up, I never knew I was waiting to be found."

Ted was obviously moved.

"And you didn't come after 'Little Guy Mike.' You came after me. I guess I've been waiting my whole life for someone to come after me."

Ted stared at the hand-written letter, finally understanding what his father had done.

Clay was on foot making his way down Cliff Falls Drive. He spotted a pay phone at the gas station. Reaching into his pocket for a dollar, he approached the gas station attendant.

"Can I get some change?"

"You'll have to go inside."

Clay walked to the cashier's window; however, as he approached, he saw Burt paying for gas.

Panicking, Clay clenched his duffle bag and, turning, raced back towards the church.

Ted glanced out the window and saw him. He got up from the booth and ran outside. He called out to him. "Clay!"

Clay stopped in his tracks. Visibly shaken, he looked to Ted. "He's here…"

Ted recognized the fear in his eyes. It was the same look from all those years ago. Clenching the letter in his hand, Ted said, "Let me get you out of here."

Chapter Twenty-Four

Ted swung open the weathered barn door. "I didn't know where else to take him."

Reagan stepped inside as Ted closed the door. Dust kicked up as the light seeped in through the splintered wood. It had been years since Reagan had set foot inside the old barn.

His eyes were distracted by the canvasses that lined the walls. He had known of Diego's artwork, but these paintings were mesmerizing. He couldn't take his eyes off them. This ramshackled barn felt holier than the church he'd built.

Ted called out for Clay, but he was nowhere to be found.

Reagan stared at the weary eyes in the paintings. "We shouldn't have left him by himself."

"He couldn't have gotten far. I'll find him. I promise."

Ted turned to leave.

"Wait…" his father said quietly, turning his attention away from the paintings. He called out for Clay.

Responding to Reagan's voice, Clay emerged from the upper rafters.

Ted exhaled.

"How did he find you?" Reagan said. "I took every precaution to protect you."

Clay glanced at Ted below.

The accusation did not go unnoticed. Reagan looked at his son having not considered the option.

"I swear it wasn't me." Ted needed them to believe him. "Whatever our differences, you have to know I wouldn't do that."

Clay couldn't figure out how else Burt could have found him. He tossed his bags below and climbed down the wooden ladder.

"Don't do anything rash," Reagan said.

"Fishing boats go in and out of Half Moon Bay, right?"

"I believe so," Ted responded.

"I can hike through the mountain pass, blend in with all the other hikers, and make it there by nightfall."

"It doesn't make sense to try to leave now," Reagan insisted. "Just stay the night. If you still want to go in the morning, I promise I won't stop you."

"I know Burt. He's not going away."

Reagan wasn't about to let him go without a fight. "We had a deal."

"You left a few things out of that deal." It was obvious

that Clay was referring to Ted.

Ted took a defensive posture. "I just saved your ass."

Reagan interjected. "Please…"

"Do what you want, but my hands are clean." Ted walked away frustrated. He knew he could never win.

"You two have more in common than either of you realize," Reagan said. "You know growing up under a microscope does something to a boy. It can stifle his voice."

"You bet on the wrong guy. Why can't you see that?"

"We're leaky, wooden vessels, Clay. That's all we are meant to be. The only words that matter are the ones that flow from the cracks in our spirit, through the breaches in our resolve. I wish I had known that all those years ago."

Clay stared at the tortured paintings planning his escape.

"Tell me, Clay, how does a man change something he's spent a life creating? A church…a son…."

"I can't do this."

"You already have."

"You don't get it. I'm not safe. Burt is probably on his way back here right now. By tomorrow, my face could be plastered on every media network across the globe. You have no idea what I've done trying to find an ounce of peace. What I've done trying to reclaim every fragment of myself that is out there…. But that doesn't matter now. Nothing I do matters…." Clay stared at the canvasses that surrounded him. "I can't escape it."

"I'm going to let you in on a secret," Reagan said. "No one escapes it. No one escapes life."

* * *

Ted was several feet outside the barn, in his hand, the letter Clay had written his father. In all the confusion, he had forgotten to give it to Reagan. He glanced over it again, the sentiment fresh in his mind.

"Until you showed up, I never knew I was waiting to be found…I guess I've been waiting my whole life for someone to come after me."

The air caught in Ted's chest. Maybe that was the answer? He took his cell phone out and started dialing.

The answering machine played. "Hello, this is Quinn. I'm probably in class right now. Please leave your name and number, and I'll get back to you."

"Quinn…could you give me a call. Tyler misses you. I miss you. I'm not mad anymore."

Quinn picked up the phone. "Ted? I just walked in. Is everything all right? Is Tyler all right?"

"Yeah, he's fine. I've been thinking about you…about us. I want to see you." He clenched the letter in his hand. "I'm taking the Red Eye tonight."

"Aren't you preaching in the morning?"

"I don't care about that anymore. I don't." He took a deep breath, preparing his next move. "I'm coming for you." Ted waited in the awkwardness of the silence.

She cleared her throat on the other end. There was a

long pause. "That's not a good idea." Her voice was small but strong. "Not now." She paused again, "I know you are having a hard time right now Ted, but I can't do this anymore."

"But I thought that this is what you wanted." Ted's shoulders slumped.

"I did," she paused, "but that was a long time ago, and now I need to figure out what I really want. I hope you understand."

"Yeah, I understand." Ted hung up.

* * *

Unlocking the door to her studio apartment, Becky tossed the keys on the coffee table beside the wilted sunflowers. She had made it back to the Acorn to finish her shift, but the other waitresses told her to go home and that they would cover for her. Even the senior waitresses offered to split their tips. Becky thought she was holding it together, but her eyes gave her away.

The red light flashed on the answering machine. As long as Becky didn't answer it, she could hope it was an explanation. It wasn't like she had known him that long, but his sudden departure made her question her instincts, and her instincts were one of the few things left that she thought she could trust. That was why she didn't regret not telling him she knew about his past. Because it didn't matter; she knew that wasn't who he was. She wanted to get to know the real Clay.

Becky pressed the button, but the message was from her brother, Max, asking her to reconsider re-locating with his family. "Hey, pumpkin…. Chicago isn't that cold in the winter…. So I'm exaggerating. But we want you to come…. You're not in the way…."

Becky glanced at the sunflowers drooping in the glass vase on her coffee table. As the message played, she picked them up and threw them in the trash.

* * *

Fog rolled in over the majestic Santa Cruz Mountains as night fell. Clay had been too afraid to step outside, so he just waited up in the rafters with his duffel bag and backpack at his side until it was dark enough for him to leave. He felt like the world was going to consume him.

He stared at the moving fog through an opening in the shingled roof, occasionally catching a glimpse of the star-filled sky.

* * *

Ted checked on Tyler, who was asleep in bed. At the boy's side, his asthma inhaler, baseball cards and a handheld video game scattered across the *Toy Story* bed sheet. Placing the items on the nightstand, Ted tucked the blanket around him and kissed him on the forehead.

He went to the closet and took out Tyler's church clothes for the next day, a crisp white shirt, khaki pants and navy striped tie. He hung them on the door.

As Ted turned to leave, Quinn's photo caught his eye. He knew she was done. He turned out the light and shut the door.

* * *

The glowing computer monitor illuminated the darkened office. Logging on, a new email was discovered. The subject line read: "Congratulations, you are the highest bidder."

Opening it, the picture of the prize won was enlarged, a rare "Little Guy Mike" Halloween Mask: Price $322.

Scrolling the page, the highest bidder glanced at the seller's name: ClayHeart, Wichita, Kansas, and a link with the familiar instructions: "Contact seller to arrange payment."

Clicking on the seller's link, the highest bidder began to type. "As usual, I will send you a cashier's check. However, I am relocating, so please hold shipment until I forward you a new address."

Staring blankly at the screen, the highest bidder proceeded to shut down the computer, but not before he was surprised by the seller's instant message reply.

"That will be fine. I hope this helps complete your collection. Clay would be happy to know he has such a devoted fan."

Clay rolled his eyes, the Halloween mask obscuring his reflection in the monitor. Although it was a risk leaving the barn, he needed to take care of business while he still had access to a computer. He glanced at the computer screen clock. It read 11:30 PM.

"Business must be good if you have to work this late. What is it, 1:30 AM in the morning there?"

"I don't mind. I get a lot done this time of night," she typed. "Besides, work doesn't keep me up as much as it keeps me company."

"May I ask you a personal question?"

"You're my number one buyer. You pay the light bills around here. What's the question?"

Clay always managed to buy a few items a month to help support his mom, scraping together whatever income he made. He was ashamed to admit that after all these years, he was still supporting her. She may have abandoned him, but for some reason he couldn't do the same. He typed his question.

"What kind of child was Clay?"

"What do you mean?"

"I've read the tabloid stories. I've heard the wild rumors. I've listened to everything everyone has had to say, but this site says that you're his mother—so do you mind if I ask you what kind of child was Clay really?"

"*Daily Variety* once wrote that when Clay was on the *Bob Hope Christmas Special* he was the only child who could keep up — "

"Before that...before he went to Hollywood. Was he ever just a kid?

His mother stared at a photograph on the wall. "Yes,

he was." She and Clay sat high in a tree laughing. They both looked young. "We both were."

Clay tried to remember her youthful face. Only now did it occur to him how young she was.

"Back then it was just the two of us…" she typed, glancing at the inventory of *Little Guy Mike* auction items surrounding her computer. "Sometimes it still is. People blame Clay, but I wasn't the best mom. You sound like a sincere young man. You must have had a good mom."

"I don't think I realized it at the time," Clay paused, his fingers over the keys, "but she did the best she could."

Staring at the computer monitor, he thought about revealing his identity, but hesitated. One day he might be strong enough to reach out, but for now, this was as close of a connection as he could make.

"May I ask you another question?"

"Sure."

"Do you ever regret leaving him in the hands of his handlers?"

"Every day…every day…And I told one of them that again just the other day."

"What do you mean?"

"This Mr. Cummings came by when I was putting together my packages for the post office. I kept telling him I don't know where Clay is and that I don't want him to keep coming around anymore, but he never listens." She continued typing. "He offered me money, just in case I hear something. But I told him I didn't need it. Not when I have great customers like you supporting me."

"He knows about me?"

"Everyone knows about my highest bidder."

Clay felt a chill race through his body. Burt must have figured it out from the addresses on the boxes. He shouldn't have risked it so soon.

* * *

Clay made his way back to the barn, covered in the blanket of night. Opening the weathered door, he stepped inside. There was no light pouring in through the fractured wood now, only darkness.

He tossed his bags in the back of the truck and hopped in the driver's seat. Reaching under the dash, he attempted to cross the wires in the darkness. As the twisted wires made contact, a blinding flash enveloped him. Clenching his eyes, he heard the passenger door open as the engine rumbled.

Turning his head, he didn't see a figure, only a lens. The second flash of light.

Clay felt the truck sputter. Pressing on the pedal, he revved the engine, but it was too late. The engine stalled. The third burst of light.

Pulling the door's handle, Clay jumped out of the truck. Retrieving his bags from the bed of the truck, he turned to leave, but he was cornered.

Burt was between Clay and the barn door, readying his camera.

"This is too perfect. It's like our own private session."

Gripping his bags, Clay backed up in the darkness, trying to fade into the hidden canvasses that surrounded him.

Burt aimed his Minolta into the darkness. "These are going to fetch a mint."

Clay cringed with each shot of the camera; each flash was like a lash against his being.

The hidden paintings illuminated with each burst of light, a vivid backdrop to each contorted pose. The violent red and purple strokes igniting like fireworks.

Clay couldn't catch his breath. He tried to hold himself together, but it was no use. He wished he was stronger, but something about being in the presence of this man made him regress. All he knew was that whatever it was that it made him feel, it was the opposite of beloved.

He dropped his bags. He couldn't escape it.

In the darkness, Clay tripped over his duffel bag and fell to the ground, the flash of the camera brightening the fear in his eyes. Here he was again, helpless.

"Leave him alone."

Clay looked up.

Burt flashed again.

Diego stood at the entrance of the barn. "I said, leave him alone."

Clay felt ashamed that Diego saw him like that.

"This is private property," Diego said. "I'm calling the cops."

"Go ahead, call the cops," Burt said, "and then everybody will know where he is."

Diego looked at Clay who had panic in his eyes.

"That's all right, I'm done here." Burt turned to leave.

Diego was between Burt and the door. "Give me the camera."

Burt scoffed at the request.

Diego pushed Burt up against the truck. "I said give me the camera."

Diego took the camera and, still holding Burt up against the truck, deleted the images from the memory card. "It's okay, Clay. You can go now."

Burt watched in disappointment as each humiliating picture was erased.

Clay grabbed his duffel bag and backpack and then turned to run out the door.

"Go ahead and run," Burt said. "That's all you do. That's all you'll ever do."

Clay stopped and looked back. "All this time you were chasing me, I may have been running from my life, but so were you Burt…so were you."

Burt's shoulders slumped under Diego's grasp. "I'll catch up with you…. The things you do, the things you've done…they don't go away. I'm always going to be there to remind you."

As Diego held Burt off, Clay Grant ran into the night.

Chapter Twenty-Five

The High Hope sanctuary basked in the brilliant morning sun. Bells rung out as the people entered the church.

Ted stood at the pulpit, ready to begin his message, waiting as the camera readied into position. He looked nervous. Reagan had scheduled the dedication of the memorial garden the same day, so even though they had announced that Ted was preaching, the sanctuary was packed. Looking out into the crowd, Ted searched for his father.

Reagan sat in the empty balcony under the jagged crack in the ceiling. He didn't want to make Ted self-conscious or take attention away from him. He thought he had slipped in unnoticed, but then he heard the familiar voice behind him.

"Can I sit with you?" The boy stood a few feet away tugging on his tie.

Normally, Reagan would insist that he sit up front, but given the circumstances, he made an exception.

The staff sat together in the first few rows sharing doubtful glances as Ted's face filled the Jumbotron.

Ted gripped the crumpled piece of paper, filled with Clay's thoughts. He looked up from it and began to share Clay's words.

"I've never had an accurate perception of God."

Ted finally spotted his father in the balcony beside Tyler. He kept his eyes locked on Reagan for a moment.

"When I was a boy…God was a kind, yet distant grandfather. Loving, but disengaged."

Reagan reached over and patted Tyler on the shoulder.

"When I got older, I perceived God as an unsympathetic IRS agent fixated on my flaws and always hot on my trail."

The congregation shared knowing smiles. Ted had made a connection.

"Apparently, I am not alone in that perception." Ted continued, a bit more confident in Clay's words. "How we perceive God has everything to do with how we perceive ourselves. So it's no wonder that I've never had an accurate perception of myself.

"A distant God has left me lonely and insecure. A critical God has left me fearful of living. I can never please either one." Ted stopped and glanced at the page, realizing he wasn't the only one who felt this way.

Reagan stared at his son.

"I've spent years numbing or outrunning those voices of condemnation that I can't get out of my head.

"But who does God say that I am? He calls us His beloved children."

Ted continued to share Clay's words, and to his surprise, the congregation was actively engaged. The words he spoke resonated, the feelings and thoughts he felt inside seemed to lift the words off the paper.

The staff listened intently, surprised by Ted's candor. Ted had humanity in his eyes and a passion that had been missing. And besides, these words were ministering to them.

Taking a long stare at the crumpled paper, Ted delivered the final thought.

"In wearing our mask we reject our true self and betray the humanity entrusted to us." The image of Clay's mask flashed in his mind, but instead of Clay's face, he saw his own. Ted paused and then repeated his last line, saying it for himself this time.

"…In wearing our mask we reject our true self and betray the humanity entrusted to us…."

Clay's words penetrated Ted's own heart. He stood there for a reflective moment as they sunk in.

Pushing Clay's message aside, he stepped away from the pulpit. In the stillness of the sanctuary Ted could hear his own breath.

He stood there vulnerable and transparent before the congregation. Then it happened. Ted Mitchell found his own words.

"Is it possible to be standing still and discover that you've been running all your life?

"That you're surrounded by people, but are in hiding nonetheless; unwilling to share that piece of yourself because it's just not safe.

"And how do you stop running when you're not even moving?"

Looking at the faces across the pews, he asked the question. "What do I want to hear from the pulpit? I want to hear that I am welcome. Not the person you want me to be or the person I often pretend to be, but the person that I am. Is that person welcome…here at this table?"

Ted moved to the rustic communion table. It was bare, aside from the basket and ceramic cup upon the folded cloth. The carved inscription read "Do this in remembrance of me."

He stared up into the balcony at his father and son and the jagged crack that skirted the central beam. It was what he always saw when he was in the pulpit, but somehow it meant something different to him now.

"See, He knew we'd forget. So at this table He says, 'My children…my beloved children…remember, I was human…I was human.'"

* * *

Immediately following the service, Ted received a crowd that waited in line to congratulate him, but he was unaffected by the praise. For the first time it just felt good to be comfortable in his skin. It wasn't that he was ungrateful. He just realized that this wasn't about him or, at least, not him alone. With each handshake and hug, he felt a connection with the people that he had never experienced before. It was an acknowledgement of each other's humanity and a quiet promise to never forget again…or at least to try.

Tyler cut through the line and stood proudly by his father's side.

Ted put his arm around his son's shoulders. He knew what Tyler would be thinking: that somehow because he'd done well that his mother would come back. Ted knew he would have to talk to him sooner than later.

Reagan remained in the empty balcony. The dedication would begin soon, but he wanted to wait as long as he could to give his son his moment in the spotlight. Pulling back the tattered curtain over the stained glass window in the back of the balcony, he squinted as the sun poured in. He was missing Rose, but as he stared at his son below, it was like a piece of her was there.

The staff looked on in amazement.

"That wasn't the Ted I know," Max said discreetly to the other staff members.

"I didn't know he had it in him," Alexis replied.

"I didn't know he had anything in him," Monica said giving thumbs-up to Ted in the distance.

"Are you still leaving?" Thomas asked Monica.

"Hell, yes," Monica said. "This week the crowd is

waving palm branches, next week they could just as easily crucify him. Honestly, what are the odds that he can keep this up?"

"You're probably right," Max conceded, but couldn't help admitting to himself that he was inspired by what he had witnessed.

Harper, an elder and organizer of the church's annual golf tournament, approached Max. He was holding a clipboard. "We still don't have a Chairman for the High Hope Golf Classic. I was hoping we could count on you." Harper held out the clipboard to Max.

"That's not until spring, right?" Alexis asked, knowing of Max's plan to leave.

Tyler was milling the crowd looking for Clay.

"Hey, Tyler...," Max called out. "I need a caddie. Are you interested?"

"Can I drive the cart?"

"We'll talk." Max signed his name as Alexis and the rest of staff looked on in amazement.

Ted was distracted as he continued to receive people. He was looking for someone in the crowd as his dad approached.

Reagan smiled with pride at Ted's success, trying not to gloat about being right about Clay and Ted.

Ted smirked, realizing that his father was either brilliant or incredibly lucky, probably a combination of both. He discreetly whispered to his father, "Did you find him?"

Reagan looked to Diego who was standing several feet away.

Diego shook his head, no.

"Do you think he's gone for good?" Ted asked his father.

"I don't know. I don't know."

* * *

The dedication of the memorial garden had come to an end. It was late afternoon, and everyone had cleared out.

The High Hope truck rumbled as Diego pulled into the upper church parking lot. As he rounded the bend, he spotted Ted and Tyler having a conversation in the distance.

As Diego hopped out of the truck, the boy walked toward him gripping a wrinkled tie in his hand. All the joy at seeing his father succeed had evaporated. Diego crouched down beside him.

"My mom's not coming back. My dad just told me."

"Did you think she might?"

"I just thought if my dad did a really good job...." The boy caught himself. "Clay was right; it doesn't work that way."

"What I like about you, Tyler, is that you just keep going."

"I know it's not my fault, but I wish I could fix it. Why does everybody leave, Diego?"

"Just know that no matter whoever comes and whoever goes, you're never going to be alone. Why don't you help me unload the truck, and then we can go to the Acorn and get some dessert."

Tyler tossed his tie in the back of the truck and hoisted himself up. Looking in the bed of the truck, he discovered a duffel bag and backpack. The boy's mouth fell open in amazement.

"Have you ever had Tiramisu?" Diego grinned.

* * *

Sunday nights were quiet at the Acorn. The breakfast crowd was long gone and those who stopped by after the dedication had returned to their homes and families.

The counter was empty. The rustic faces of city workers and ranch hands depicted in the art-deco mural were like guardians keeping watch over the town, the bold colors and idealistic message of brotherhood were more apparent in the stillness.

Becky was putting out the setups for the next day. She stared at the spoon, watching the colorful light from the cellophane toothpicks overhead dancing in the reflection.

"The owner just called. There is a private party here tonight," the waitress said to Becky. "Would you work it?"

Becky glanced at the clock. Her shift was ending soon, but it wasn't like she had any real plans. "Sure…"

She had a standing invitation for dinner at her brother's, but that was his family time, and besides she didn't want to hear about whatever plans they had for moving to Chicago.

Tossing the rag on the counter, Becky stepped into the kitchen and was surprised by what she discovered.

Clay stood in the doorway holding two grocery bags and a bouquet of sunflowers.

Becky didn't know if she could trust what she was

looking at. "What are you doing here?"

"I got as far as North Beach. And then I realized you've never had Tiramisu. It just didn't seem right."

Clay managed to hand Becky the sunflowers. "These are for you. They're a pitiful bunch, really."

Becky looked them over.

"I just had a feeling that in the right hands they might have a shot." Clay set the bags on the counter. "I got everything we need." Reaching into the bag, he removed each item he had purchased at the Italian store in the city: flour — the good kind — coffee beans for the espresso, cocoa powder and brandy. "The right ingredients matter if you're going to make the real thing."

"And you plan on making all this here?"

"I have permission." He smirked.

Looking over her shoulder, Becky saw the waitresses gathered about, smiling.

"And most important: we have the right recipe." Clay tore a piece of the brown paper bag with the recipe scribbled in pencil. "I called a special friend and she convinced her dad to give it to me."

"A special friend?" Becky squinted, looking suspect.

"Don't worry, Bella's only ten. By the way, she says hello."

"You told her about me?"

"Yeah…and she gave me some good advice. Actually, something I had told her. I'd repeat it but it really doesn't make any sense unless you're hanging from a rope."

Becky rolled her eyes. "Just because we have the right recipe and the right ingredients…it still doesn't mean it's going to turn out all right—"

"There is so much about me that I'm afraid that once you find out you're not going to like. But this time I'm here to stay."

"You're not going to disappear on me?"

"I have some unfinished business in Kansas, only a couple of days, but then I'll be back."

He held up the wooden spoon. "Bake with me…?"

Becky's eyes welled up with tears. "Don't tell me how, but I knew you'd come back."

"How could you know? You don't really know me."

"Maybe I know better than you think."

Clay looked at her, puzzled.

The "Closed" sign sat in the window at the Acorn. Whatever threat was out there, Clay was no longer going to waste his life running.

Clay and Becky were covered in cocoa powder, laughing as they stood before the stainless steel bowl. As she gripped the wooden spoon, he reached around and placed his hand over hers, and then guided her as she folded the egg whites into the mascarpone mixture.

Glancing at the rustic faces in the mural and the promise hidden in their eyes, he was still unable to reconcile the idealistic message of brotherhood with the truth about the paintings in the barn.

"What is it?" Becky said, noticing the curious expression on his face.

"I wish I could sit down with the artist who painted

that mural. I think I could learn a lot from him."

"But you know the artist…"

Looking closer this time, he spotted something he had missed before: the artist's mark in the lower right hand corner: "DXM."

He had seen those initials before. "Of course, Diego…"

In that moment he knew he was exactly where he was supposed to be. Despite everything that had or would happen, he was staying put. That much he knew. He glanced at the cellophane toothpicks overhead. It was a glimpse of Heaven.

Continue the journey at

clifffalls.com

- Discover more about Cliff Falls and find out what others are saying

- Explore *Beyond the Falls*

- Communicate with the Author

- Follow us on Facebook and Twitter

- Purchase additional copies of *Cliff Falls*

- Find out the latest news about *Cliff Falls*

* * *

*For information about having the author speak to your group or organization, please contact: **office@clifffalls.com***

ACKNOWLEDGMENTS

This is a book about belief, so it is only fitting to thank all of those who were not only a part of this project, but who believed in the story—and me—even when there was little evidence to support what I was doing. What they have in common is that they are not just talented but are good people with generous hearts, and they are but a few of the faces that I see in the mural above the counter at the Acorn. I am proud to walk among them.

In the fall of 1996, I went over the falls in my own life when a health challenge landed me in bed with little more to do than write. This story was part of a restoration process that was years in the making. It had several incarnations, first a television pilot, then a screenplay, and finally, a novel. I don't plan on writing an opera, so hopefully the book did the job.

This novel would not exist without my mom, Marie Anne Shiepe. Belief is a powerful thing. From day one, she believed not only that I could do it, but that it would be healing for people who read it. Her gift of belief is unending and allows all those around her to believe in a loving God. I am grateful for her support, as I am for the continued support of my father, Clifford Shiepe, and for the encouragement of my sister, Bayne, and brother-in-law, Jose Meza.

Ron Glosser, a mentor and friend, has done everything he can to encourage me. He and his wife Lilly are two of the most sincere people I know. I am so blessed to call them friends.

Nancy Ellen Dodd has been my trusted editor for every phase of this project. A gifted writer in her own right, she has an amazing ability to take my words and arrange them in an unexpected way. I am so grateful for her friendship, and for the way she always reminded me to never cut anything that meant something to me.

Jeremy Rivera is a brother and a best friend. A gifted speaker, he paints with words and calls people to a more sincere walk with God. He brought great insight to the confession scene and has been a sounding board not just for the book but also for my life. He is one of a kind and pours his heart into everything he does. One real friend is worth a thousand imitations.

Maureen Saliba has a gift for logic and believability that I relied on throughout this project—often that included endlessly reading passages over the phone until we were both confused. Whatever challenge was before me, she never hesitated to jump in and to see if she could help. That's the kind of person she is.

Kevin Collins stretched me as a writer. Always acting with a willingness to speak into this project, he was less concerned with what I wrote but why it was important. Kevin will push you to that ultimate truth even when you want to pull your hair out. But he was right, and the story and I are better for it.

I want to acknowledge my team of first readers who gave me their thoughts and feedback on the manuscript. Each contribution was significant. Thanks to Charles Slocum, Paul Petersen, Sarah Skibitzke, June Scobee Rodgers, George Taweel, Bill Lawrence, Tricia Collins, Molly Nonnenberg and Fr. Francis Mendoza. Special thanks to Doug Binzak; Mark Yameen; Michael Marchand, who always told me to keep writing; and Action Hero Jorgen De Mey, who was part of my physical restoration that shadowed the writing process.

I also want to thank Brennan Manning, whose writings have greatly impacted my life. The line "In wearing our mask we reject the true self and betray the humanity entrusted to us" was greatly influenced by Brennan. If he didn't write it, he probably should have. Thanks also to Amy Grant. I was lucky to hear "Find what you're looking for" prior to its release, and it inspired me to revisit the courtroom scene. Thanks also to Michelle Katz and Steve LaVoie from Art Center College of Design, and Brad Cummings for their helpful advice. And to the good people at The Dutch Goose and Mike's Pastry, and to George Hamilton, all of whom gave me permission to use them in the novel.

Michelle Hubele is my talented line editor—and newly discovered distant cousin. Thanks to my creative team: Sean Teegarden for his inspired cover design, Jane Moon for her thoughtful interior layout, Tim Holl for website design, and Pam McComb for my photo on the back cover. I appreciate all of their time and dedication.

Above all, I want to thank the One who has seen me through. "After you have suffered a little while, He Himself will restore you and make you strong, firm and steadfast." Whatever that looks like, I'm game.

* * *

Going over the falls will change you, but how it changes you changes everything…

* * *

Beyond the Falls: Share the Experience

Note from the author

The touchstone of the *Cliff Falls* experience comes full circle when you invite others into it. Who do you know that needs to be reminded, or perhaps hear for the first time, about the truth of where their value comes from? What faces come to mind?

As this book continues to change lives, our hope is that it will be shared with others. Consider the following options below to share your *Cliff Falls* experience:

SHARE & CONNECT

- Visit *Beyond the Falls* at *www.clifffalls.com/ beyondthefalls* to engage with the author and to learn about upcoming events and appearances.

- Share your insights, discuss the book with other readers, and get the latest news from our Facebook fan page: *facebook.com/clifffalls.*

- Get updates and communicate with the author on Twitter. Follow us at *twitter.com/clifffallsbook.*

· Your recommendation is a powerful thing. Review us on Amazon.com. Talk about the book on your online networks. Write about us in your local paper, favorite magazine or website. Request the author as a guest on your favorite radio show or Podcast. Contact people you know who have a voice others respect; ask them if they would review a copy and make some comments on their website, newsletter, etc. Help create buzz.

· Word of mouth gives life to a book's success. Tell your friends about this book. If you have a website or blog, share an insight about how *Cliff Falls* impacted your life. Visit *www.clifffalls.com/promote* for information about linking to us.

GIFT / RETAIL

· Purchase additional copies of *Cliff Falls* to give as gifts to friends, family, even strangers. A fast and cinematic read, this story is a wonderful reminder about the truth of where our value comes from. Visit *www.clifffalls. com/shop.*

· If you own a shop or business or run a community program, display these books in a prominent location. We give discounted rates at *www.clifffalls.com/shop* for anyone ordering volumes of six or more.

* * *

*For information about having the author
speak to your group or organization, please
contact: **office@clifffalls.com***

* * *

.